D1562507

Spooky Basement 3: The Final Pumpening

Clay Astroman

For Cool Idiots
www.spookybasement.com
www.forcoolidiots.com

Art by Neil Astroman: www.iceandshadows.blogspot.com
For Cool Idiots
ISBN: 9798617332805

"Tear it up! You know we gonna tear it up!" *–Bébé's Kids*

Dedicated to Kästle. <3

Urth
(Shitty Apartment, 3 AM)

"Dude, watch out!" Baron yelled as a bulbous, pallid creature leapt from behind a crate and latched onto his best friend in the universe or galaxy—whichever is bigger.

"Fucknockers supreme!" Garindax shouted in agony as a pair of gleaming fangs and three pairs of fungusy fingerfangs dug into his frets.

The guitar/spider monster electrified his razor-wire strings in an attempt to shock the attacking creature, but it wasn't very effective.

"No good!" Baron called. "It's a Chomorian! That means it's half electric-type, half spicy-type!"

Garindax panicked, but only for half a frigg'n second before he flipped his pickups to reveal *lipstick* pickups on the other side.

1

"Baron, play something!" he shrieked. "And don't worry, lipstick pickups are real things that make guitars sounds cool and surfy. They DON'T mean the guitar or the player wears lipstick."

"But how can I shred?!" Baron demanded from a cage strung from a chandelier made of holographic skeleton arms. "I'm in this cage made of holographic skeleton arms!"

"Dude, it's a puzzle! Look at the pinky on the green skeleton arm! It's blue! Switch it with the pinky on the blue skeleton arm!"

Baron switched them, and the cage evaporated. As he fell to the slimy stone castle floor, he held out one hand. And one guitar pick.

The pick gravity-strummed Garindax's strings and sent a chill-type surf attack coursing across his reversed pickups.

It was *super effective.*

The chill-type attack nullified the spicy-type defenses, and the Chomorian fainted.

Baron and Garindax immediately drew dicks on every square nanometer of the creature's face. What made it even worse/better was that the alien from the Chome Galaxy had swim-team pictures the next day, so he spent hours scrubbing his face with a washcloth in an attempt to remove them.

What made it even worst/best was that it didn't work, so in the picture his face was covered in red, irritated dicks that he foolishly told the rest of the team he "spent the *ENTIRE* night trying to get off."

It was the ultimo bust, and the ultimo adventure, and the ultimo stopping point for the night.

Baron removed his VR headset and Garindax's custom VR headset that had eight tiny lenses for his eight tiny spider eyes.

Planet Urth came back into dim, sickly-yellow focus.

"Maaan, that ruled!" Baron sighed as he crashed both headsets back onto their docking stations.

"No joke!" Garindax sighed back. "I wish the real world could be as sweet as nerd-game world."

"Yep. Doesn't it feel like it *used to be*? Like, didn't we used to have way more adventures?"

"Uh, does fucking 'Monsteropolis' mean anything to you?"

"Dude, it means pretty much everything to me—especially after we got past Mrs. Bones."

"Oh, yeah, that's where the real meat/pump began. If we had decided to stop our adventure at

Mrs. Bones, it would've seemed pretty superficial up to that point. But, oowee, did the party go off. And P.S., what about Christmas Cingdom with two C's?"

"Eh, it was mostly bullshit," Baron replied. "It was a *solid* adventure, don't get me wrong. Worth the price of admission. For the most part, though, it was pretty *un*-pumped. That fucking guy we were with, 'Doug'? What was his name? 'Dougie'? 'Douglas'? He was a little bitch."

"True. I think it was 'Pink Dougie,' actually."

"Pink Dougie Ashley. That was definitely it. What a baby."

"But, hey, we still got something out of it because, in the end, you got your pump back. That's not a spoila because you were there and that shit is finished."

"*How Baron Got His Pump Back...*" Baron whispered. He flexed, and tiny little veins sizzled across his knuckles. "I'm still pretty pumped, too. So, why did we stop adventuring/killing? Is it because we started playing too many nerd games or eating too much soy lecithin or something?"

Garindax started to respond, but suddenly the apartment door exploded open, and the sound of cackling exploded into the room.

"Haha oh my frog, bitch. That bartender was such an asshole!" one of the voices laughed.

It bellowed from a goth chick. She was still mostly babe, but you could tell she used to be *more* babe. She wasn't a mom, so that meant her body was still tight, but she *was* a "proud mom of ten pugs," with the bumper stickers and crewneck sweatshirts to prove it. That tempered her babeness a bit—and Baron's pump.

She was Baron's wife, Lulu.

The two still did "stuff" every now and then, but not nearly as much as when they got married, and not nearly as much times infinity as when they were dating. The thing Baron used to most look forward to with her were his birthday beejes. "Birthdeejes," he called them. But then once, and only once, he farted during a birthdeej.

It was silent and stink-free, so he probably could've gotten away with it, but he kept giggling until Lulu finally asked what was up. He only told her because he thought she would think it was funny, but she *didn't*. And his honesty/mistake blew out the literal fucking candles on that and every future birthday. He was now lucky to get a birthday bathroom sink heej, which he referred to as "birthroomseejes" with unshared delight.

"Girly-bitch, he was only acting that way because he was *into* you!" the other voice laughed. "He was ALL up on the clit!" This voice came from a chubby dude with a graying high-and-tight haircut.

He was Garindax's husband, Mussie.

Mussie used to run marathons and be super ripped when Garindax met him at a home-and-garden show, but now he was super dumpy. And for some reason, or maybe *for* this reason he drank a shit-ton of powdered lemonade in a reused water bottle.

He and Garindax still and only ever did super-quick peck kisses because that's all they ever saw on TV.

"Ooh, you think?" Lulu said coyly while setting two bags on the counter. Wine bottles and wine boxes clattered loudly, causing Baron's teeth to clench. "Bitch, should we go *back?*"

Baron's pump dropped.

He reached for the VR headset out of habit/comfort but then quickly withdrew his hand. He knew he would get in trouble if he used it while Lulu was home and he was supposed to be doing dishes or helping her decipher meme text through her shattered phone screen.

"Ooh, bitch, you are *bad*," Mussie sang while doing a little shimmy. "Let's change, get a couple of chocolate martinis in us, and then get a couple of pistachio bartenders in us. That means they're Italian. Because pistachio is typically one of the three flavors in Neapolitan ice cream, bitch girly."

"Dude, why did we get married again?" Baron whispered quietly to Garindax so their spouses couldn't hear. Luckily, by that point both of them had sashayed down the hall, wine bottles in hand. The wine boxes remained on the counter, cardboard omens of another loud/terrible night.

"I think because we were bored and didn't know how to use the microwave."

"Oh, yeah. Well, fuck-fart that. It's time to get *un-bored*, and then maybe on the way home get some tacos that are *already* microwaved."

Baron swung Garindax over his shoulder and headed to the door. As he grasped the handle, two shrill voices shrieked, "Um, EXCUSE YOU?! You're not going ANYWHERE!"

Urth
(Shitty Apartment,
3:15 AM,
Maybe Grounded)

Baron turned to face his wife, who was now wearing half as much clothes. Half as *many* clothes? She was doubly naked.

"But me and Garindax were going to hit uh, Chore Store and Errand Depot," Baron lied. "To get you both gifts and do chores."

Lulu narrowed her eyes. "Too fuck' bad. Mussie and I are drinking tonight, so you need to stay home and be ready to come pick us up when we tell you to. And don't even *think* about picking us up in your dumb little jet shoes. Use the sedan. You'll need to clear some shit out of the back first. And fill it with gas. And get the state inspection done."

"But me and Garindax…"

"Hey. Asshole. Don't make me do *The Face*," Lulu warned. She began to crinkle her nose and narrow her eyes even more. It was something she had seen on a 90s sitcom that made 90s sitcom husbands super scared.

"Oh no, not *The Face*!" Baron said through gritted teeth. An attempt to take the path of least resistance, as usual. It didn't work, as usual.

"Don't you spectrum smile at me, boy-o," Lulu snarled. She grabbed Baron's right nipple and twisted it.

"We both know *The Face* isn't really a thing. But what *is* real is how scared you are of me. And you *should* be. Same for your little friend. You're both on thin-fucking-ice. And if Mussie and I leave the two of you, you'll have no one. Honestly, who else *would* want you? Your face smells like a VR helmet, and he's a guitar/spider monster that smells like a VR helmet. Now get out of my way, and be ready to pick us up when we tell you to."

She pushed past Baron, opened the apartment's front door, and stepped into the dimly lit hallway.

Mussie followed, leaving a toxic trail of perfume like the Mad Gasser of Mattoon.

Garindax pursed his spider fangs for a TV peck, but his husband sauntered right past him. "Have a fantastic night, little nerd game babies!" Mussie huffed haughtily.

The door slammed shut.

Garindax unpursed his fangs, and Baron wondered if he should start dishes or laundry first. Sometimes the hot water heater got fucky, so he needed to be strategic about it.

Urth
(Shitty Apartment,
3:17 AM,
Def Grounded)

"Hey, man, fuggit," Garindax said to break the silence throbbing through every square inch of the apartment's asbestos walls. "Let's crack some 64-minute BBIPAs and get back to EFSM VR."

Baron trudged back to the couch and picked up the VR headset. He knew he would soon be in a colorful world of pump, noise, and distraction.

Escape from Sideburn Mountain VR. Escape.

Escape from Lulu and bills and his job at the carpet outlet and dogs that he tried to be cool with but that never seemed cool with him. He wondered if that meant something was broken inside him, since dogs were supposed to be cool with everybody. Was he uncool? Was he sick?

Could they smell it? Some dogs could apparently smell that sort of thing. Was he dying? How long did he have left?

"Press start, mang," Garindax called from somewhere far across the room, but also inches across him in a virtual lobby.

Instead of a blacker-than-a-witch's-butthole spider guitar monster, he was a whiter-than-a-yeti's-taint gorilla saxophone monster. One of his arms was an alto sax, and the other was a tenor sax, so he could play *any* Kenny G song with relative ease. It was totally out of character for him, which made sense because it was a video game character.

Baron pressed the start button and saw his character come into frame. An ultra-ripped metal musician jet-booted onto the screen. His eyes were full of fire and life. Baron refocused his own peepers and saw his sad, tired real eyes reflect in the VR lenses. He refocused on his character's, and then on his own. The crows' feet made his stomach drop.

"Hey, you're not doing that fucking eyeball thing again, are you?" Garindax said pissedly. "Don't torture yourself, man, just chill. Slash, sip, and kill stuff with me."

Baron closed his eyes.

"Okay, Garindax. I'll slash/sip/kill with you. But guess *frigg'n what?*" He took off his headset pissedly. "This time it's going to be FOR REAL. You know? Like when that dude goes, 'Welcome to Fright Night—FOR REAL. *That* level of intensity. I'm only going into detail because it may have been hard to see my face or totally hear me because you still have your headset on. Just in case something was missing, like if you were reading or something and couldn't pick up on subtle stuff like tone. Anyway, just imagine the Fright Night dude saying that line. Because I appreciate that you are more comfortable with movies than reading, and I don't judge you for that because I'm the same way."

"Man, fuck reading," Garindax said pumpedly while taking off his headset." Every book should come with a free video game and a slightly awkward but totally genuine handshake."

"FUCK READING—FOR REAL."

"FOR TONIGHT ANYWAY."

"Ooh, Night of the Demons ref?" Baron asked.

"Yep!" Garindax replied. "Eat a bowl of fuck reading! I am here…to *PART-EEEEE!*"

"Haha! Dude, you should write *that* in a book."

"Okay."

Urth
(Sweet Neon Streets,
4:20 AM)

"Man, I can't believe we just frigg'n bailed!" Garindax cheered as he and Baron jet-booted over Urth's sweet neon streets at 4:20 AM.

"Believe it, homie," Baron said. "I'm done having virtual adventures. It's time to have legit adventures again. So, we're going back to where it all began. AKA where it all pumpgan: *PizzArea 64*."

Baron and Garindax crash landed in front of PizzArea 64. It looked almost the exact same. It was shining like crazy with a fresh coat of mercury paint, and lights were flashing to get you Pete and Pete for Halloween or Christmas. The only difference was now it had gray hair to let you know that time had passed.

Baron and Garindax busted confidently inside.

"Oh bonsoir, bebesitos!" a French voice cooed upon their arrival.

It was a maître d at the PedCheck gate, just like before, only now with a Spanish accent/influence. Not in a bad way, just in like a "people fuck more readily and internationally because of technology and global infrastructure" kind of way. In that sense, it indicated that time had passed more effectively than gray hairs on a pizzeria.

"Are you boys here to partake of un peu de 'za? Or perhaps you fancy los videojuegos?"

Baron remembered when/why he impudently killed the last maître d with a razor guitar pick. It seemed kind of schticky now. He felt that he had evolved.

"Oh, but do go fuck yourself, my good/dark probably-a-ped," Baron said while pushing through the PedCheck gate without so much as an apology or a blacklight stamp, the latter of which he later regretted not snagging.

The maître d obliged and began frantically fucking himself, oozing moans and various slimes all over PizzArea 64's neon carpet as Baron and Garindax busted into the main lobby.

"Man, you've really evolved," Garindax said proudly to Baron.

"Thanks, homie. Now, let's kick this party off with un peu de fucking 'za. We don't want to go back to Monsteropolis on an empty stomach."

"Def not. But are you sure you want to go back there? Don't you want to go somewhere *new?* You know, we had been talking about going to Sideburn Mountain and doing a camping thing."

"Yeah, we were *going* to, but then those news reports came out. What'd they say, that all of the camp counselors turned out to be ped monsters? It just seemed too intense, so we bailed even after sinking time/money into the plans. I mean, it's not that peds would've tried anything with us, and certainly not that we would've been peds for going, but we just can't be associated with that ped-heavy of an adventure."

"Oh, yeah. Remember how much shit people gave us after Monsteropolis just because like ten of the monsters happened to be moms? Everyone was fucking Freud all of the sudden. We don't *have mom* issues; we *had momster* issues. Big difference. That said, you sure you don't want to go somewhere different? Honestly, man, fart Monsteropolis."

"Yeah, but Christmas Cingdom, AKA Kristmas Klandom, wasn't any better. Plus, if we go back there, we can't even go to Pumphalla Video because we never returned *Bebe's Kids* or *Earthworm Jim*, so the late fees would be killer. Double plus, it's not like anyone is watching our adventure or counting on its novelty, so fuggit. This is just another day, like going to the dry cleaners. Which, shit, we need to do before Lulu gets home. But for now, let's eat some 'za, kill some obese chef monsters, and maybe hit up a monster hotel for some M64 games."

Baron and Garindax busted up to the food counter, where a teenage girl with an upside-down visor didn't greet them since she couldn't see them through her plume of ass vape. This, too, wasn't necessarily bad. It was just indicative of another natural progression. Kids loved poop emojis, so as they grew up, the next step was teens who wanted nothing more than to directly inhale a fog of feces directly into their lungs. Baron understood, so he didn't get pissed.

"Tick Tock! Tensley boomer cashapp?" she asked as they approached.

Baron didn't understand, so he got pissed.

18

Still, he maintained his cool in order to prevent offending the cashier and ruining his entire life.

"Excuse me, please and sorry, and I hope this meets with your present gear system's, um, fancy. But I'm afraid I presently do not understand the depth of your most impressive and important, uh, discourse."

"I know what chop means," Garindax blurted less tactfully. "So chop-chop, bia-bia."

The girl gasped a thick plume of fogces and stormed into the kitchen.

Suddenly, the metal doors exploded open and she reappeared, sobbing atop a mountainous obese chef monster with a high-and-tight haircut and face tattoos.

"You boys sexually assaulting my employee?!" he interrobanged. "Can't you tell from the color of her shoelaces that she is currently in an INTJ, cat-with-seasonal-depression gear system? This means she is *NOT* open to your advances—nay, your *impositions.*"

"Dude, when did obese chef monsters get so lame?" Baron whispered to Garindax. "Is this because of CBD?"

"Hey, they're all still red on the inside," Garindax said with eight winks.

Baron shredded a quick progressive metal riff, and Garindax's eight winks reopened to shoot eight lasers that replaced all of the chef monster's sparrow and nautical compass tattoos with vulture and dragon tattoos, which were a definite improvement.

The chef began to sob uncontrollably because his sparrow and compass tattoos represented how he was free to chart his own path in life, and now they were gone. His tears combined with the teen worker's to produce a torrent of hyper tears that rushed toward the duo, who continued doing a much sweeter kind of wailing.

Thinking quickly/pumpedly, Baron swung Garindax down and used him as a surfboard right before the tear tsunami crashed into him. As he got pitted, so pitted, he cranked the reverb on Garindax and wailed a horror surf solo that summoned a parody Cthulhu monster from the depths of the weeping wave.

The chef and teen died instantly upon seeing the horrific sight since the dude who created it (H.P. Lovecraft, not Baron) was racist.

Baron coasted to an ice-cool stop. He then grabbed some popcorn from a nearby machine, scraped some of the saline tear residue off

Garindax's fretboard onto it, and busted into the kitchen with his newfound snack/glory.

Inside the kitchen, there were no more obese chef monsters or teen workers with their own unique gear systems. Instead, sterile-stainless steel robots churned out pillars of pizza while also selling "big data" about kids' topping preferences and vom contents.

Baron snagged a couple slices of FauxFuture meatless pepperoni pizza that was half-soy-lecithin, half-CBD, but somehow nutritionally deadlier than normal pepperoni pizza. But that was fine because Baron had a tenuous attachment to life, and Garindax just didn't give a crap.

The duo busted back into the Ballerific Birthday Blastorium, ready to chow down.

Even though pretty much everything in the kitchen was now automated, robots had been removed entirely from the BBB's stage show. Instead, TVs with terrible refresh rates that were either too slow/choppy or too fast/buttery showed videos about pissed eight-year-olds who were really good at debate or worried about plastic straws or something.

"Oofa," Baron exclaimed with a mouthful of pizza. "What happened to this place?"

"What, PizzArea 64?" Garindax replied with fake pepperonis stabbed over his fangs.

"Nah, Urth."

"The kid on TV is saying that it has something to do with straws or bees," Garindax responded worriedly.

"I dunno man. Either way, it sucks. Maybe it *always* sucked, and we were just too young and dumb to notice?"

"Dude, we were just here like two years ago," Garindax reminded him. "It ruled then, and we haven't read or gone to school since, so I'm pretty sure we're just as dumb."

"Then maybe everything else changed? Is that possible? Can straws do that? Kids don't want the same stuff as their parents because most parents are assholes, so stuff *has* to change in order to sell. But I'm a parent, or I was before I wished my kid away, which I guess does make me an asshole. So, my stuff went away, too. But will it come back? 'It' meaning my stuff, not Dougie. What if I do nice stuff like that TV show with the dog who had to do good deeds to not be a dog?"

"Dude, stop saying and thinking about 'stuff' so much," Garindax said. "Just relax and enjoy your grossza. The fake pepperonis are solid/spicy.

Scrape the goodie off. Besides, some new stuff rules, like VR, while that dog show was old and sucked fucking pp."

Baron felt a twinge of guilt.

"You're right as usual, homie," he said. "Even if everything turns into fake pepperonis, I can always count on you for a pump-up. Just wait till we're back in Monsteropolis. Everything will be sweet then."

"Dude, remember what your therapist said. You're not supposed to say 'I'll be happy when…' You gotta be pumped/present in the moment."

"Impossible."

"More like *un*possible, meaning you're able to turn that shit on and off. Do that trick she taught you. Where's your pissed/bummed level at?"

"Prolly like infinity."

"Okay. Well, name five things you see."

Baron tried, which is what counted.

"1) A standup arcade game of *Infant Shark Runner*, the phone game based on that stupid song for babies, standing where the *Escape from Sideburn Mountain* beat-em-up used to be. 2) Mold on the ceiling tiles. At least it's probably OG mold. 3) A vom stain on the carpet. It's *definitely* OG vom because it's purple from when they used to have Grape Ape Executioner in the soda fountain. 4) Pizza. 5) You."

Garindax smiled a spider fang smile. "Good, dude, good. Don't forget to breathe deeply between each one. Through your belly. Make that innie an outtie. Now, four things you hear."

"1) Some redemption game yelling '*Bingo!*' over and over again. It's kind of annoying, but kind of familiar/pumped. 2) Wooden skee-balls being chucked overhand into the hundo hole. 3) Some kid getting his ass beat by his mom, probably for overhand chucking skee-balls into the hundo hole. 4) Smooth-jazz/rap artist Lil' Wobbly Penisi on the house speakers. It's his number-one hit: *Slappin' Buttz and Bustin' Nutz*. Radio-edited version, but still solid."

"Most excellent. Exhale. Three things you feel."

"1) A pocketful of tokens. Mang, I'm glad this place hasn't switched to a bullshit card system yet. 2) A/C blasting like crazy. 3) Pizza in my hand. It tastes better than it looks."

"Nice. And on that note, two things you taste/smell."

"1) Pizza. 2) More pizza. It's actually pretty frigg'n good."

"Okay, finish him! One thing that's a true fact *right frigg'n now.*"

"I'm just…chilling in PizzArea 64," Baron said matter-of-factly.

"Where's your pissed/pumped level at?"

"Like, 31."

"See, dude? Way better than infinity. And if we did it again, you'd prolly be at like an ice-cool 13."

"Thanks, homie, but there's no need. I feel a lot better now."

"Hell yeah. Then lemme 'axe' you this: Are you ready to hit up Monsteropolis and get *real pumped, real quick?*"

Baron didn't even have to answer.

He and Garindax busted out of their booth and over to where Big Scooter's Lil' Scoots' Ball Pit used to be—where it always had been—both of them now feeling pretty baller. That is, until they came across a sign that read in QR code, "Welcome to Doc Scooter's Lil' STEM Scientist Learning Lab, Sponsored by Booshani Bottled Water."

"What the fucking FART?!" Baron screamed. "Dude, it's gone! The ball pit is gone!" He tore into the lab but found only shitty indie games, a rocket ship ride that gave you dual college credit, and some colored pencils because it was actually a STEAM lab, which meant it included art and everything but needed a special name to sound innovative for the hand-wringing mamas and papas.

Garindax ran biometric scans and saw that Baron was in not just trouble, but double trouble. His pissed/bummed readings were off the charts.

"Yo, I know this is bullcrap," Garindax said calmly. "But let's try grounding again and figure it out."

"I tried, man," Baron said gravely. "Oh, man, did I try. I tried grounding. I'm already grounded. I'm grounded here. I'm grounded at home. My entire life is grounded/r-worded."

Baron zombie-walked over to the STEAM lab's rocket ship ride: "Let's Get Sirius (AKA Let's Go to the Garage and Listen to a Little Satellite Radio [in the Car])."

He climbed in and plunked a token into what strangely looked like a tailpipe even though it was in the cockpit.

The dash blinked to life.

"Dude, please," Garindax pleaded. "Just try it."

"Okay," Baron said calmly. "Five things I see. 1) The colored lights on the ship's control panel. They're…getting brighter."

Outer Fucking Space (What Is Time, But a Miserable Pile of Secrets?)

A familiar voice chuckled somewhere in the dark. Baron's eyes opened and saw an obese face morph into static on a coin-operated CRT TV across from him.

He looked to his left to see a sign with a glowing bus schedule. *Does that say "Chocolate World"?* he thought. *There's no way.*

To his right was a ticket counter with a cashier that looked like he was made of porridge. The cashier had a worried expression on his lumpy, pasty face, and his gaze was fixated right above where Baron sat.

Baron looked up and saw a 7'-tall, sour gummy worm mufucker looming over him.

"What the shit?" Baron groaned.

The gummy worm smiled and turned to reveal a blacker-than-butthole guitar/spider monster slung across his back.

"Garindax!" Baron yelled. He tried to get up, but two other sour gummy worms that he hadn't even noticed were holding him down. One was neon blue with green stripes, and the other one was neon green with blue stripes. They were also mufuckers.

"Slooby! Slooby!" the duo of dulces gurgled. Sour sugar crystals fell onto Baron's black shirt, making it look like he had dandruff when he definitely didn't.

Baron turned his head and chomped into both of them. Even though it was gross that they were alive, he wasn't afraid of gummies.

"Bootenzo!" the blue one shrieked.

"Blue razz. But of course," Baron smiled as he spit the blue candy onto the ground because it turned out he actually was a little scared of it.

"No blastas!" the porridge cashier shouted.

The green worm released Baron and panic-slimed back into the wall. Baron stood up and bit into him, but not in the neck or mouth or crotch or anywhere weird.

The gummy worm shrieked something else cool/nonsensical, like, "Schnabu!"

"Sour apple abobo," Baron said as he spit out the chunk and the worm shriveled and flopped onto the other now-dead one. "But of corpse."

"Don't you mean, 'sour apple *adobo?*'" a voice called from the bus stop entrance. It came from a mega babe. She had shoulder-length, dyed gray hair that made her extra babe because at first glance Baron was like, "What's this fuckin' old bag doin' here, eh?" But that's when he noticed her porcelain face and unblemished olive skin, which looked like she wore a bunch of makeup but really she just stayed out of the sun because she was too busy chilling in her room writing fanfics about Monster in My Pocket.

Her eyes were as gray as her hair and kind of crossed, which just made her more endearing and kinda sexual, as if she were permanently looking at your thang while—

"Here, let me help you up," she said, interrupting Baron's fantasy.

"Thanks, but I need a few seconds," Baron replied for obvious reasons.

She leaned over and grabbed Baron's rip, which meant she only got around like half of a tricep. Baron noticed how her jugs were bigger than expected considering her slim frame.

Could they be implants?

No.

They jiggled freely beneath her gray v-neck shirt, which almost chilled his boner for a second because between her gray hair, eyes, shirt, jean shorts, and fishnets it was almost like she was trying *too* hard. But that's when he noticed that she used black eyeliner as boobliner to make her cleavage line more prominent/intense. This also made her look like a cel-shaded video game character, which made Baron rebone so hard, he pre'd.

"Uh, what were you saying?" he said to buy time.

"I was saying that I think you meant sour *adobo*," she replied. "Like, the Mexican spice."

"Nah, I meant 'abobo' like 'Abobo.' You know what that's from?" Baron asked confidently.

"It's from Double Dragon," he continued before she could answer because he was too impatient but also too pumped to share his cleverness with her.

"Mmm," she replied while biting her lower lip. "I like that game. I like the kid who rollerblades."

"Haha nice," Baron said less confidently. He knew that she was actually thinking of Skate from Streets of Rage 2, but it was okay but that was still a good game. Besides, she just said "the kid who rollerblades" instead of using a racial descriptor, which showed that she was civil. But she also didn't give an impromptu TedX talk about *why* she didn't, which showed that she was chill.

Baron's pump/bone maintained.

"Want to go save my best friend/guitar/spider monster with me?" he asked.

"Sure," she answered with a wink. "I'm not scared of spiders or obese chef monsters."

"That's a strange and deliberate thing to say," Baron said warily.

"I myself am strange and deliberate," she replied while raising her eyebrows and looking around like she was in a haunted attic.

Baron's pre became a post.

He stood up, grabbed one of her fishnet-clad cheeks (butt, not face), and stuck a finger in one of the holes (fishnets, not butt).

The duo walked out of the space bus stop, prepared to rescue Garindax and kill any gummy worm mufuckers that stood in their way.

Outer Space (But Specifically, AKA "Pacifically," Outside a Space Bus Stop Somewhere)

"So, where are we?" Baron asked coolly despite the fact that he was on a foreign planet and Garindax had been kidnapped by a sour gummy worm.

"You're on Planet, uh, Bookcase," the chick replied less coolly.

"You don't sound very confident. Did you just make that shit up because there's a bookcase store across the street?"

"No, this is definitely Planet Bookcase. It's in the, um, Computer Speaker Galaxy. Part of the Box-of-Tissues-for-Masturbation Nebula."

"That's pretty complex, so I believe you," Baron said with a nod. "What is a nebula, though? Is that bigger than a galaxy?"

"I don't know. My name isn't Google, bitch," the girl snapped.

"Whoa, okay. Chill. What *is* your name?"

"It's Seeree."

"Cool. Like the Apple thing?"

"No, it's spelled differently and either totally unrelated or a parody. Plus, I'm definitely of age and not a minor, so my parents named me Seeree before the Apple thing that I won't spell just in case. But I came first."

"How could you get sued if you came first?" Baron asked.

"Hey, ask anyone facing a paternity suit."

"I…don't follow."

"Because the dude came first. That's how babies are made. If the girl goes first, then she can't get pregnant. That's what my last boyfriend told me, anyway. But, extra-anyway, it was just a joke. What're you, dumb?"

"No, my name is Baron."

"I know who you are," Seeree said.

"Whoa, that's crazy and dramatic," Baron gasped. "How?"

"Because," she sighed, "I'm your daughter."

"Whoa, please tell me that's a joke, too."

"Nope, so, you might want to stop pinching tips."

Baron immediately yanked his hand out of his pocket and put it over his mouth to indicate his surprise—but not *too* close. Because only seconds before, he had been pinching tips.

"Let's go grab a drink," Seeree said seriously. "I'll explain everything."

Outer Space (Bar Full of Aliens Playing Brass Instruments)

"Okay, so how are you my daughter?" Baron asked as he pulled out a convoluted bar stool that had to be unscrewed from the ground because it was in an outer space bar full of aliens playing brass instruments.

"Sex," Seeree replied matter-of-factly. She pressed a button on the underside of the bar, and bubbling purple drinks materialized in front of her and Baron.

"Yeah, but I mean, who is your mom?"

Baron raised one of the drinks and took a sip. It tasted like someone made Ghoul-Aid using gin instead of water, i.e., perfect.

He continued, "I've done sex to a bunch of babes. One in Monsteropolis *and* another one in, uh, fucking Christmas Land. I can't remember what it was called. What's the ABV on this bad boy? I think it was called Kristmas Kingdom. But then it turned into Christmas Cingdom. Shit, I just caught that it wasn't K*h*ristmas Kingdom, like with an 'h,' even though it had one when it was when it started with a 'C.' That's really going to bother me now. Fuck."

"Dude, I don't know," Seeree said pissedly. Her drink was already gone, and she was jamming on the button beneath the bar to order another. "You think I asked my mom where you fucked her?"

"I dunno, maybe. Or she could've just been spamming about it because I was so good. What's her name, at least?"

"Mom."

"Oh, yeah. I forgot every mom is called that. What else can you tell me about her? Like, what does she look like?"

"She's, I guess, kind of goth. Pale skin, black hair, rad jugs."

"Dang, that's both of them."

"Yeah, I don't know what to tell you. Where the fuck is my drink? This lag sucks."

"Have you ever seen her boobs?" Baron asked.

"No, not since I was a baby and sipped from them," Seeree responded.

"Hmm. One had a single hair coming out of the nip, so that would've been a good tell."

"That's a pretty gross tell, ashley."

"Ashley? That's her name?"

"Actually. Are you going to finish your drink? Give me that shit." Seeree snagged Baron's drink.

"Sure. Did you grow up in Monsteropolis or Kristmas Kingdom?"

"I only remember growing up here, on what'd I say? Planet Bookcase? I might've been born somewhere else, but my other dad got transferred here for work when I was a tiny baby-baby."

"Your *other* dad? What the shit? What's his name/problem?"

"I just call him Dad 2. He's in the murders and executions industry."

"What a douche. Do you have any siblings?"

"Just one. An older brother. A brother…with shockingly feminine bosoms."

"Oh, *FUCK*."

"His name is Dweem."

Outer Space (Bar Full of Aliens Playing Brass Instruments, But Now They're on Break, So It's Quieter/ More Intense)

"Your brother is Ultra Slaughterhouse—I mean, Dougie—I mean, DWEEM?!" Baron said while mashing the button under the bar because Seeree was killing his drink, and he desperately needed another.

"You know it," Seeree belched. "He's a real asshole, too."

"No frigg'n joke! But how is he *alive*? I thought I un-existed him with my one, true Christmas wish! I even saw him disappear right before my eyes, and right before Santa started stacking and jacking it. How is he not either dead in the lamer version of Pumphalla, Bishasshalla, or back in my nuts as an unborn baby?"

Seeree looked up with glazed eyes and whispered with booze breath, "There are more things in space and earth, Dad, than are dreamt of in your philosophy."

"Oh shit, you know about Urth?" Baron said. "And isn't that quote from that frigg'n Insane Clown Posse song? Are you a jugalette? Fucking hell, do I have an asshole son *and* a jugalette daughter?"

"No, it's from William Spacespeare."

"Haha, so dumb."

"But to answer your question and get us back on track," Seeree slurred, "I don't know. Dweem is way older than me, so he's just always been around. And as long as I've known him, he's never mentioned anything about a Kristmas Kingdom. Nor a Christmas Cingdom."

"Unsurprising, the ungrateful frigg'n chub. It was a solid adventure, and the only family trip we ever took. It was a little more intense/depressing than Monsteropolis, sure, but still a lot of fun and worth the like $10. I'm still pissed that Garindax and I didn't get to chill with Big T. Frost, though."

"Who?"

"Big T. Frost. He was this, like, gorilla clown monster Santa. See, there were all of these bullshit Santas, but also a couple of sweet ones, and BTF had to have been the *sweetest* one, but we didn't even get to meet him because Dweem got his sock wet and freaked out. But it was just frigg'n sweat, and then this jester elf monster was like—"

"No," Seeree interrupted. "Who is Garindax?"

"Oh, fucknockers!" Baron gasped. "We gotta go save my precious homie/your uncle!"

Big Outer Space (3 AM)

Baron busted outside and onto the neon streets of Big Outer Space, where he now realized he was because he was leaving an alien bar and because there were UFOs everywhere, which technically *weren't* UFOs because Baron immediately identified them *as* motherfucking UFOs, so they were technically motherfucking FOs. MoFOs.

As Seeree opened the door to follow him, Baron heard a rimshot and a bunch of laughter at what must've been a terrific joke being told by the standup comedian alien who had taken the stage. A delightful portmanteau, perhaps.

"Dad, waitaminute!" Seeree called from the doorway. "It's not safe out here at night!"

Baron was about to ask how she could tell it was night in outer space, when suddenly a giant pink hand grabbed his shoulder and squeezed way too hard to qualify as a massage.

Big Outer Space (3 AM and 10 Seconds)

"You shouldn't have come to outer space, you filthy hume!" a gruff voice grunted in Baron's ear. It reeked of bacon and mayonnaise.

Baron spun around and found himself staring into a pair of beady red eyes. Then he realized they were actually a pair of chafed nipples, so he looked up a few feet into the beady red eyes of a pig/man/alien. He was wearing a cop hat because of course.

Seeree ran out onto the sidewalk as another rim shot and the sound of laughter followed from the closing door. The standup comedian was killing between the portmanteaus and vivid storytelling.

But she'd have to catch his act another time.

Still holding onto Baron's shoulder with one hand, the pigmalien reared back his other, which was as big as a ham hock since it was one.

Baron tried to swing Garindax around and wail a thrash melody to melt the pigmalien into that pink sludge stuff that turned so many kids off of chicken nuggets and lined the pockets of so many poofy-haired, coked-up charlatans who like to scream at children in elementary schools and hit on divorced assistant principals that they hope will financially take care of them. But Garindax still wasn't there, so Baron just wailed an air guitar melody that didn't do shit.

"Welcome to Big Outer Space!" the pigmalien snorted as he brought a honey-baked hoof crashing down into Baron's face.

Big Outer Space (3 AM and, I dunno, like 16 seconds)

The pigmalien's fist exploded into a mist of red blood and pink sludge right before it connected with Baron's mouth.

"*Squeeeeaaaaoowwww!*" the space pig shouted. He pulled back a stump with a bone jutting out of it. It was covered in teeth marks as if a dog had been going nuts on it. But it was actually Baron who had been going nuts on it because he loved gross fast food.

"Heh heh," Baron laughed as he licked slime off his lips. "I guess my air guitar still…cooks. Or, wait. I guess my air guitar is like an air fryer. It is hot but you can't see/understand why."

The space pig collapsed to the ground, to reveal Seeree standing behind him.

Her hands were up and her nose had a single drop of blood coming from it.

"Whoa, are you some kind of psychic STEM major with telekinetic powers?" Baron asked.

"...Yes."

"So, my air guitar didn't do shit?"

"No, that was all me. I'll admit it. I fucking love science."

"Damn, how cool/original, especially because you're also kind of no-nonsense. But now I'm 1000% sure you're not my kid, Maury, because Dweem was dumb as fuck. He only passed remedial math because his teacher once called him r-worded in class and we threatened to sue. Plus, I only took your mom to the Bone Zone once. Her name's Leila, by the way. And if Dweem is your *older* brother, then that means you're not twins who 2P co-op came out of her."

Seeree did the math in her head for fun and confirmed that Baron was right. There was no way he could be her dad.

"You're right," she sighed.

Baron immediately began re-pinching tips.

Back in the Space Bar (2 Space Beers Deep)

"How could Mom lie to me?" Seeree said. She swirled the head of her space beer in its glass, thinking about viscosity and volumetric pressure and other STEM shit.

"She's kind of a bitch like that," Baron said while jiggling his glass to make the head of his space beer dance around like an idiot. "One time, she told me my VHS copy of Ernest Scared Stupid got eaten by the VCR, but then I saw the cassette chilling in the trash like someone had taken a hammer to it. And on top of it was a hammer and like three things of my pumpkin English muffins. They weren't even spoiled, either, because they were from my freezer stockpile."

"That sucks about the English muffins, but I have no idea what Ernest Scared Stupid, a VCR, or a VHS are."

"Oh yeah, how old *are* you?" Baron asked.

"Old enough," Seeree said with sly grin.

Back at Seeree's Place (2 Urth Balls Deep)

Baron and Seeree did a sex, boobs and everything.

Seeree's Bed
(Just Chilling)

"So, now that we did a sex," Baron said while exhaling space weed, "I guess you probably shouldn't call me 'Dad' anymore. Like, it was cool *during*, but now it'd be kind of weird."

"Definitely weird," Seeree said while exhaling a sigh because she was feeling unfulfilled and kind of irritated. "But I can't call you 'Baron.' That's what my mom always called it when we had to take poops. 'Making a Baron,' she'd say. How about 'Dad 2'? Is that kosher?"

"Wow, lame. But nah, we should prolly leave out the 'Dad' part altogether in case we want to kiss with tongues or something in public. How about 'Dad 2 D2'? No, fuck, that still has 'Dad' in it. What about 'D2D2'? Is that cool?"

"It's definitely not 'cool,'" Seere snapped, "but I'm getting tired of this conversation. So, sure.

But now the question is who is my actual dad? Mom's new husband, Randy?"

"Oof, I dunno," Baron responded. "He's a vampire, right?"

"Yeah."

"Well, then, I'd say probably not, because you certainly didn't display any sucking skills with me tonight! Hey-oh!"

Baron looked to Garindax for approval, but Garindax was still kidnapped by sour gummy worm aliens. He then looked to Seeree for approval, but got fucking zeeeeero.

"Fuck you, D2D2," she scoffed. "Just for that, I'm calling you Baron. My mom was right; it's apt nomenclature."

"Well, call me what you want, even if it is Zack Nosferatu Creature. I actually kind of dig that. Either way, I'm going to go take a Baron and then save my precious homie. You coming?"

"Not ten minutes ago, not now, and not ever."

"Whoa, that was pretty good! You sure you're not my kid? Fart, I hope not. Alright, I gotta shit."

Cruising in Seerees' Hoversedan (Blasting Lil' Wobbly Penisi Because Urth Radio Signals Reach Outer Space)

After making some waffles with straight-up coffee beans in the batter, Baron convinced Seeree to rejoin his party. There was even a cool little jingle that played.

The duo then busted out in her hoversedan in search of Garindax.

"So, who were those gummy worm monsters that kidnapped Garindax?" Baron asked while they blazed by billboards advertising hologram lawyers and laser colonics.

"Neon skworms," Seeree replied. "One of the many confectious creations of your son, and my brother. Well, I guess he's my half-brother now since you're not actually my dad. Which makes all of those erotic folk metal songs he recorded about me a little less creepy. Not a lot, but I'll take it."

"Dweem?" Baron balked. "He makes gummy worm monsters? That dude couldn't even make oatmeal without starting a fire. The only saving grace was he always cried enough to put it out."

"Yeah, well now he's the most powerful obese chef monster this side of the Box-of-Tissues-for-Masturbation Nebula. He started off babily, by curling 20s and making chocolate petit fours. But before you could say 'big frigg'n whoop,' he was curling 50s and making cinnamon pedophiles."

"Pedophiles?"

"Spicy ones."

"Wow. And, I guess more importantly, why?"

"Who knows? He simply creates monsters and vomits them onto the world without regard for how they interact with—or hurt—anybody. He thinks it's funny, I guess. He's basically a bored, immature malcontent. A real dick."

"Sounds like it."

"Which is why we're going to have to kill him."

Chilling in Seeree's Space Sedan (At a Drive-Thru Window After Politely Asking for Five More Mild Sauces)

"Kill him?!" Baron choked with a mouthful of fried space chicken.

"Yep, Dweem has to go," Seeree replied coolly. "He's terrorized this planet long enough. At first, I let it go because I thought his creations were pretty harmless. But then I started seeing their effect. And I'm not just talking about, like, the neon skworms who strangle people from the esophagus-out, or the baklava bots who steal people's identities. A few weeks ago, I saw this little chubby kid with a bowlcut playing in the sand."

"The *space* sand?"

"Right, the space sand. Anyway, he was forming what looked like gingerbread men. I asked what he was doing, and he said he was making gingerbread men."

"Whoa, that's def fucked up."

"No, it's not. He was doing exactly what I thought he was. Are you even paying attention to me? Stop fucking drumming on the window for a second and listen! Damn."

"Sorry." Baron chilled.

"Anyway, he said he was making gingerbread men. And I noticed he was putting these little black pebbles in them—jamming them deep into the center of the pretend pastries. I asked if they were chocolate chips, you know, as a top-secret bonus treat? He looked me right in the eyes, but only for a second because I think he was uncomfortable with eye contact, and said, 'No…they're raisins.'"

"Gross. But still not as bad as dead flies," Baron replied while raising a finger. "At least my son ain't no Gordie Belcher. *'Gordie Belcha, you lardass!'* Do you know what that's a reference to?"

"Shut up! But keep listening. You were doing so well."

"Okay, sorry."

"It's not important *what* they were," Seeree said, "it's important *why* they were. When I asked him why he would hide raisins in a cookie, he said, 'Because people hate them. It's funny. Like DweemBig&BeBig on F-You-Tube. Now are you planning to whip those jugs out, princess, or what the hell are we doing here?'"

"Oh man, I forgot about 'Dweem Big & Be Big,'" Baron sighed. "That was such BULLSHIT."

"Well, it continues to spread like the virus it is. Dweem's streaming channel has a quintoxillion subscribers. Every video has a two-minute intro, ads every few seconds, and cuts after every word. It's super jarring. But whether he's making nougat tigers or driving around in a hovertruck while spewing diatribes about caramel as his face gets progressively redder, he always brings it back to how his creations are meant to fuck with 'normies.' Since everyone thinks they're special and everyone else is consequently a 'normie,' the viewers eat it up. It was bad enough when he was just creating candy monsters, but now he's creating *obese chef monsters.* Spawners. His growth is exponential, and I'm not just talking about his belly. Dweem has to be stopped."

"But isn't it too late, then?" Baron asked hesitantly. He hoped it was his time to talk and maybe start drumming on the window again. "What about all the baby chef monsters?"

"If you kill the head obese chef monster, all of the babies will fry eggs. That means die. I thought I may need to specify since they're chefs who may, at times, *literally* fry eggs."

"Damn, are you sure you're not my kid?"

"Yeah, it's just something my mom used to say. She must've gotten it from you. But we've already established that I'm not your kid. I made sure of that at the $p < .000001$ level before we did a sex."

"Okay, cool. Then how about some road head?"

"Sure," Seeree replied sensually.

Baron unzipped and kicked back, but nothing happened. Then he remembered that Seeree was driving. He looked over at her.

"Get to it, bish," she said while keeping her eyes on the space road but also fully unzipped. "And wipe that mild sauce off your lips first. Wait, actually, don't."

Baron got to it.

Cruising in Seeree's Space Sedan (After Getting to It)

"So, what's the plan to defeat Dweem?" Baron asked confidently after delivering another round of spicy pleasure.

"First, we have to collect the 7 Pumpedly Pins," Seeree said frustratedly after receiving another round of mild disappointment. "Once all of them are attached to my gray leather jacket, I'll have enough power to fry Dweem's eggs. I think maybe I'll castrate him to death."

"Oofa! Glad I'm not that guy! But can't we just go rescue Garindax, and then I'll wail a couple of power chords to beat Dweem's ass? Or, honestly, I don't even need Garindax for this. I'll just give Dweem a little slap across his hamster cheeks— face *and* butt. Trust me, I remember him from when he was a kid or 30 or whatever. He was a pudgy little baby with a bowlcut and puffy, inverted nipples."

"That was before," Seeree replied gravely. "He's still obese since he likes to sample his creations, but there's no way you or your little ukulele are scratching this guy. The dude can curl like a hundo now, and do twice as many burpies."

"Dang," Baron whispered. He looked at his own biceps and wondered if he could curl a hundo. He probably could, but his form would suck and he'd be lucky to get two full reps, let alone any partials, which he and everyone knew were key.

"What about the bowlcut?" Baron asked, hoping to discover some kind of weakness. "Does he still have that?"

"Oh yeah," Seeree responded. "But now he gels it down super flat and *then* hits it with a mist of hair spray."

"Whoa…does he call it gerbil hair?"

"What the shit? No. How is that 'gerbil hair'?"

"Because it's wet."

"Gerbils aren't wet. Man, I'm glad we're not actually related. But, no, it's not like a gerbil. It's like a fucking Pachycephalosaurus."

"Dang," Baron whispered again. He wondered if pachywhatevers were more like hamsters, but he knew better than to ask. So, he changed the topic. "Does Dweem sample the cinnamon pedophiles? Because that would be a little freaky-deaky."

"Okay, you're starting to give me a headache. It's officially Shut-Up Time. Just trust me. We need to collect the 7 Pumpedly Pins. That's the only way to take down Dweem. Plus, they're good padding."

"For your jacket?"

"Sure."

Grass World
(Loading Screen)

"Why are we starting in Grass World?" Baron said as he and Seeree descended through stars, and a vivid green planet came into view.

"Because, bish, Grass World is always the first world," Seeree snapped. Didn't you say you play video games?"

"Yeah, but I call them 'nerd games' because it's funnier."

"Not really."

"Garindax thinks so," Baron said defiantly. "Anyway, what about the Space Bus Stop? Wasn't that World 1?"

"Nah, bish, that was like a hub world."

"But what about the pigmalien? We shouldn't be able to fight in a hub world."

"We didn't, bish. The pigmalien was outside the Space Bar. That was a tutorial level. And, as I recall, you didn't do any of the fighting."

"Hey, I bit his wrist bone after you exploded his hand. That probably hurt," Baron clarified.

"True," Seeree said with a condescending nod. "That's likely what *actually* killed him. Not the fact that after I exploded his hand, I telekinetically disconnected his heart and sent it on a nice waterslide through his intestines and out his b-hole. Or did you miss that part, bish?"

"Can you stop calling me bish?" Baron asked.

"Sure thing, bitch," Seeree answered.

"Maybe we should go back to Dad2D2."

"No way, you blew it just like you blew that pigmalien's bone. It's going to be bish, bitch, or Baron, but just remember that Baron means poop."

"Baron is fine."

"Cool. Let's start snagging those pins, Baron. Each one is protected by a world boss. So, all we need to do is locate and kill the boss of this world and then six others."

"No problem. Even without Garindax, I'm awesome at punching/kicking stuff, especially because I have these jet boots that I never seem to use anymore for some reason. Who's the first boss?"

"Remember those neon skworms from the Bus Stop?" Seeree asked seriously.

"The Space Bus Stop, yes," Baron corrected.

"The first boss is basically a giant version of one of those."

"Wow. Dweem is already hitting the creative wall on World 1?"

"I think he was aiming for a gradual build-up," Seeree explained. "But yeah, it's probably more so that."

"Does it at least have a cool name, or is it just something like 'Giant Neon Skworm'?"

"It's 'King Skworm,' so you were surprisingly close."

"Fucking Dweem," Baron said disappointedly. He shook his head and then looked across the grassy fields of 1-1 through 1-💀. At the top of a mountain loomed a shadowy monolith of a gummy worm. Its sour sugar crystals glistened menacingly in the sun, and on top of its head was a rock candy crown that glistened slightly more menacingly to indicate that it was even sourer.

Seeree shuddered. "Okay, let's plan our attack," she said to Baron.

But he had already disappeared.

Grass World (1-1)

Baron rushed across the technicolor, pixelated plains.

An army of tiny, acorn-looking bitchass enemies with grumpy expressions trotted toward him, but he just avoided them because he didn't need the experience points.

"Wait, slow down!" Seeree yelled while chasing after him.

"No way!" Baron yelled back as he ran up a hill and crossed a bridge. "I'm speedrunning this mufucker!"

"But look, under the bridge! There are a bunch of little acorn monsters under it, but the bridge is so wide that it isn't like Dweem put them there as a threat like, 'Yo, don't fall off or you're f-bombed by acorns.' It must be a red herring!"

"What, like a fish?" Baron asked while still running. "I thought Dweem only made candy. What's with the acorns and fish?"

"No, you idiot," Seeree snapped as she reached the bridge. "The acorns are marzipan, so that still technically counts as candy, and a red herring just means it's something put there to trick us. There's more than likely a top seeks under this bridge!"

Seeree crouched and peeked on the underside of the wafer planks, where a bunch of chocolate coins were spinning like crazy. It was probably enough for an extra life. Maybe even enough for a continue. Best of all, the coins were guarded only by tiny little acorn monsters just itching to get squished.

As she bent over to grab the nearest coin, she felt a sharp slap on her fishnet-clad, right cheek.

She shrieked and sent a telekinetic blast from her butt, but there was no stink because it was just energy waves/vapors.

Baron flew backward over the bridge, landing on a pile of acorn monsters who loved every hot second of it.

"Yeesh, what the fuck!?" he demanded while rubbing his head and wiping acorn slime off his jeans.

"We already did a sex, so why are you pissed that now I was just trying to get me a little sweet?!"

"You startled me, you asshole!" Seeree yelled back.

"Well, your asshole startled me! Right off the bridge and onto these dainty fucks."

"Ooh, can oo squish *me*, too?" a dainty fuck pleaded while nudging Baron's arm with its acorn face.

"No way!" Baron said as he elbowed it away, causing the corpse slime of its friends to smear across and into its mouth, but it didn't even care. It also loved every hot second of it.

"Hey, at least get the coins!" Seeree said.

"Nah, now they'd just be a reminder of how you assaulted me," Baron replied hurtfully as he did a one-armed pull-up back onto the bridge. "Plus, you know we need like 100 for an extra life or whatever, and fuck that. I'm not here to collect coins like some chubby banker with a wet middle part, wetter armpits, and a wettest crotch. I'm here to *slap buttz and bust nutz*, both with a z. 'Butts' and 'nuts' with a 'z,' not 'slap' and 'bust.' That'd be stupid."

Baron slapped Seeree's cheeks with both hands and then rushed up the bridge, stomping eight acorns in a row so a little *ping!* sounded across the sky to let everyone know he had gotten a one-up.

"See? Fuck a coin! Let's go save my boy and your kind of uncle boy!"

Seeree sighed exasperatedly and loped after Baron, following the trail of busted nutz.

"This is so disgusting!" she complained as she looked down and saw that her gray Chucks were covered in viscous white acorn slime that smelled sort of like chlorine.

She scanned the horizon to yell at Baron, but stopped upon finding that he was knee-deep in shit.

Sour, sugary shit.

Grass World (1-2)

Baron had been ensnared by a purple-and-orange neon skworm, at least twice as big as a normal skworm to indicate that it was a mini-boss.

"Baron!" Seeree yelled as she raised a hand and prepared to fire a telekinetic blast of skwormicide.

"I'm fine!" Baron shouted back from inside the constricting gummy spiral. "This is my brand-new friend, Skwormdo."

"Friendo!" the neon skworm gurgled happily.

"Sorry. I meant this is my brand-new friend, Friendo."

"No, you were right," the gummy worm corrected. "Skwormdo is my name. But I *am* friendo!"

"Oh my fuckness," Seeree exhaled angrily.

"Whoa! That's something else I say," Baron said while trying not to inhale too many sour sugar crystals. "Are you sure we're not related?"

"I told you that I ran the statistical analysis, and we're thankfully not. 'Oh my fuckness' is just something my mom used to say. You must have infected her, and then she infected me."

"Cool. Well, at least I didn't directly infect you. With that *or* with my wiener when we did stuff. Hey, Friendo, me and her did stuff!"

"Ooh, nice!" Skwormdo cooed while squeezing Baron tighter.

"What is with the fucking squeezing?" Seeree demanded.

"I dunno. The dude likes to squeeze, and I don't dislike it."

Skwormdo uncoiled and gave Seeree a bitchy look.

"See, now you've embarrassed him," Baron said sadly. "Friendo, just ignore her. She may know about STEM, but she knows nothing about PUMP, which stands for Pumped-Up Mama Protectors. Because you gotta love moms and not have issues with them. So coil away, mama!"

Skwormdo wrapped back around Baron and commenced to squeezing.

Seeree suddenly had a massive headache, like an ice pick was shooting through both temples and jammed into an outlet on the other side.

She closed her eyes but still saw Baron and Skwormdo, both guffawing in moronic delight while the latter squeezed the former for seemingly no purpose. She imagined how easily it would be to…end the farce. She opened her eyes and stared down at her hands and the energy that emanated from them.

A drop of blood fell onto her palm.

"Whoa, your nose is bleeding again!" Baron said, wriggling free from the gummy grasp.

"I'm fine," Seeree rasped. "This is just something that happens whenever I—"

"You're like that waffle girl from the show!" Baron interrupted. "Hey, Friendo, she can do tele—uh—telepathic stuff."

"Ooh, nice!" Skwormdo cooed.

"Yeah, but she didn't when we did stuff. She just kind of lied there. She's swirly good at doing telepathic stuff with her mind, but not with her *head*, if you catch my drift. But don't worry, I took care of business like you know your boy do."

"It's telekinetic!" Seeree shrieked. "And 'lay,' not 'lied.' I'm not even touching the fucking 'swirly' thing. But I *will* reiterate how glad I am that you're not actually my dad. Because if you were, I'd probably be as retarded as you!"

"Ooh!" Skwormdo moaned. "Not nice."

"Yeah, Seeree, what the shit?!" Baron bristled. "It's 'r-worded.' Even someone as 'r-worded' as me knows that. You're so uncouth."

"Baron, I—" Seeree started. "Wait, *uncouth?*"

"Yeah, bet you didn't see that one coming, did you? Word of the Day, bish. June 20th, 2012. Anyway, me and Friendo are frigg'n *outta* here. We're gonna go rescue Garindax by ourselves. You can stay here and think about how you ruined this entire day for everyone."

"Me?!"

"Yes, you. *You, you, you.* It's all about you. Happy now? And PS, I'm glad you're not my daughter, either, because if you were I'd have to ground your ass. C'mon, Friendo, let's bounce."

Skwormdo coiled around Baron, squeezed oh-so-tight, and bounced like a spring toward the mountain where King Skworm regally/sourly chilled at the top.

Seeree sat down sadly on the grass Indian style, or I-word style just in case.

Am I the wrong one here? she questioned.

She looked toward the mountain base, where Baron and Skwormdo were already bouncing, laughing, and now for some reason eating apples.

A drop of blood fell from her nose onto her jean shorts, a crimson blemish on her otherwise perfectly gray outfit.

She stood up. Another drop of blood fell, but this time she telekinetically caught it in mid-air and boiled it into vapor.

Grass World
(1-💀)

Baron bounced with Skwormdo up the mountain, passing a bunch of cannons and acorn monsters and stuff he didn't want to deal with because he was in a rush.

"Yeesh!" he yelled when he finally reached the peak, where a 64-foot neon sour gummy worm rose into the literal cotton candy sky. The monster was purple and green swirled, not striped, indicating that was not only a high-end gummy, but possibly a Halloween one.

"Even the individual sugar crystals on this guy are bigger than me," Baron continued. "I think we're f-bombed here, Friendo. Let's just bounce back to Seeree and see if she'll take us to a pool or something."

"Leaving so soon?" King Skworm bellowed, causing his rock candy crown to jiggle and send prisms shooting all over the place.

"Yeah, man," Baron replied. "You looked way smaller from the ground. I don't think I have enough jet boot fuel to fly up to your snout, let alone punch it."

"Then turn your tail and go," King Skwormdo said dismissively. "I only accept challenges from ultimo warriors, and you look like you skipped leg *century*."

"Ooh, don't talk about my best friend in the universe that way!" Skwormdo shouted, which caused his voice to crack and a tiny piece of apple to fly from his mouth.

Baron grimaced because he was embarrassed for Skwormdo, but also because he was embarrassed to be hanging out with him, and because now the air smelled like sour apple bites.

King Skworm gasped. "You there! I can tell you are an ultimo warrior. Do you challenge me?"

"Ooh, yes!" Skwormdo replied confidently.

"Him?" Baron asked. "He's an ultimo warrior? But I'm not? You've gotta be kidding!"

"Ha!" King Skwormdo laughed. "Of course I'm kidding. Look at him. He looks like a fish poop. At least you have jet boots and pretty okay delts."

"Hey, thanks, but also not cool!" Baron yelled while flexing his delts. "Just because Skwormdo is special needs doesn't mean you can be a jerk to him. This isn't the 90s anymore."

"It's all cyclical," King Skworm chortled. "You'll see. Bullying will come back once everyone realizes it's actually somewhat helpful. I'm only king because some nougat motherfucker called me 'sloppy' in 10th grade. The next day, I got some new regal threads, stretched myself out in a pasta maker, and then sent him and his entire family to the dungeon toot-fucking-suite. Watch, I bet your next workout is going to be legs after what I said, huh?"

"No," Baron lied.

"Yeah, it will. And then you'll look and feel better, and babes or dudes or worms or whatever you're into will be more into you. Why do you think I only fight ultimo warriors? Because I want to better myself. You can't sharpen a knife on butter. Now go squat down the mountain, lunge back up, and then burpie back down. Your pecs are crossing that line where they're more 'preasts.' You're getting titties. Too much soy lecithin, probably."

"Damn…" Baron whispered sadly.

"Ooh, do me!" Skwormdo said while bouncing excitedly. "Help Skwormdo improve!"

"Nah, there's no helping you," King Skworm growled. "You're fucking sloppy."

"Ooh," Skwormdo sighed with his pitiful apple breath. "I want to say that bums me out, but I actually have pretty low self-esteem. So, in a way, it's satisfying because it fits my narrative. Is that what you were talking about? Is this good?"

"Don't listen to him, Friendo!" Baron snapped. "You're awesome, and an *ultra-ultimo* warrior! And besides, this guy doesn't know shit. He's just a first boss!"

"What did you say?!" King Skworm roared.

"You heard me! You're probably still part of the tutorial/tech demo for this adventure! You're a French boxer with a glass jaw, or some random robot that's not even a master, or a dumb little bat monster that can't even turn into Dracula! You're a first fucking boss!"

Baron activated his jet boots, which he then realized would've been a much faster way to get up the mountain than a bouncing gummy worm. He blazed up 64 feet, wielded Skwormdo like a whip, and cracked it right into the rock candy crown, which he prayed held all of King Skworm's power.

As soon as Skwormdo connected, the crown exploded into like 100 sugary shards that stabbed mostly into King Skworm's eyes.

Baron jet-boot grinded down the shrieking, dying king, busting sweet loops and occasionally using the Skwormdo whip as a zip-line.

"Heh heh, still got it," he chuckled as he came to an ice-cool stop at the bottom, which was still technically the top (of the mountain).

"What, gray pubes?" Seeree asked. She was chilling on the redwood-sized tail of King Skworm's corpse and telekinetically removing petals from a candy corn daisy.

"Fart!" Baron shouted in surprise because he hadn't seen her/had kind of forgotten about her.

Skwormdo started barking and charged toward her, but as soon as he reached her she tied him into a knot–not even telekinetically, just with her own hands—and flung him off the mountain ledge.

"Friendoooooo!" Baron wailed. He leapt into the air and activated his jet boots, but they only sputtered. He had used all of his fuel flying to the top of King Skworm.

Baron fell to the ground with a loud *Thwok!*

It was echoed by a quieter, gummier *Thwok!* somewhere far below.

"You okay?" Seeree asked nonchalantly while plucking the last candy corn and flinging it at Baron, who lay crumpled at her feet.

"You're lucky I don't hit ladies," Baron grumbled into the grass. "And you're *super* lucky that I don't have Garindax with me. His attacks don't count as either of us hitting ladies. It's just me wailing, and then a lot of catlateral damage."

"*Collateral* damage," Seeree scoffed. "What you said is that VR video game where you're a cat who breaks stuff. But if you're *so sure* that you could teach me a lesson if you only had your precious guitar, now's your chance."

Baron looked up from the dirt at Seeree, who was nodding over her shoulder at the other side of King Skworm's corpse.

He pulled himself off the ground, staggered over, and peeked at the other side of the tail.

A tiny, one-room castle rose from the grass. Through its hard candy stained-glass window, Baron saw the shape of a headstock. His eyes widened.

"Garindax?" he whispered as hopefully and joyfully as a kid getting a Christmas present with airholes cut into the box.

"Hurry up with the reunion," Seeree groaned. "We have more worlds to hit up before we can kill Dweem. I don't want to say the number of worlds right now because it's going to sound like a lot. They'll all be pretty different, though, so it will be pump. Don't worry."

"Oof, *pump*?" Baron said as he shoved past her. "You are your mother's kid."

He kicked open the wafer door and shouted, "I'm here, precious homie! And now we can start shredding again so I won't feel so weak compared to my kind-of daughter who I did sex stuff with. But I'll tell you all about it. For now, unravel those strings and do your cool spider walk into my waiting arms. It's best friend time!"

"Oh, I sorry!" a wimpy voice called from the shadows. "But your guitar-spider-monster-thing is in another castle!"

Baron's heart dropped, and his eyes focused in the dark to see a fat mushroom alien sitting on a wooden stool and plinking on a ukulele. Its legs were crossed like a lady, and it was wearing a little penis-shaped hat. The mushroom alien was, not the ukulele or the wooden stool.

"Who are you?" Baron yelled. "A fucking bad guy?!"

"No, I'm neither a good guy *nor* a bad guy. I'm simply here to tell you stuff, and maybe hang out. My name is Spike Vegelta. But I don't like my name very much, so you can just call me 'Frog.' Because I very much *do* like frogs."

"Tell me this stuff, then, Frog," Baron said sternly. "Where's Garindax?"

"World 2. Desert World. World 2 is *always* Desert World."

"Oh, cool. That was actually surprisingly easy. Now, then, tell me this. Why do you have a little penis hat on your head? What's going on under there? A penis?"

"There is a long, storied, um, story about this hat. Allow me to regale you. The year was—"

"It's the pin," Seeree interrupted. "It's not a *penis* hat, it's a *pinis* hat. As in, the 'pin is here under this stupid fucking penis hat.'"

She knocked the hat off Spike's head, and perched atop his bald scalp in a nest of wispy mushroom hairs was a pin shaped like a grass blade with a hilt.

She snatched the pin and tossed it to Baron. "There. I just saved us like five minutes of bullshit. Put this in your pocket, and let's go to the next world.

Seeree confidently strolled out of the castle, leaving Baron totally beguiled and Spike totally humiliated.

But both of them were at half-mast.

Desert World
(2-1)

"Oh, *Desert* World!" Baron said as he and Seeree landed on a sandy plain. "I thought Frog said, 'Dessert World.' Which, if you think about it, makes more sense considering that Dweem is all about sugar monsters. But I guess that may be *too* obvious because he's all about sugar monsters. Hey, do you think the sand is at least pixie stick dust? Maybe it's just normal sand. I mean, at some point, there's gotta be a line for the candy stuff becoming too schticky, right? Is that why this is just called Desert World?"

"Please shut up," Seeree grumbled. She stumbled out of the car and began searching the skyline. Beneath the atomic fireball sun, she saw a few taffy magic carpets and baklava goblins: your typical/playfully racist desert enemies.

It shouldn't be hard to find the pin and get out, she hoped.

But her head was killing her, and her nose wouldn't stop bleeding.

She had tried correcting Baron no fewer than twenty times about the dessert/desert thing on the drive over, but as soon as she started talking, he would either ask about how she knew what was under Spike's hat or get distracted by how "baller" it was that a hovercar flew past, despite the fact that they were actually in one.

"I need five minutes," Seeree pleaded. "Can you *please* just shut up for five minutes?"

"Oh, sorry, I'm just pumped because we're about to get Garindax back. But, yeah, I'll be totally silent from now on."

"Thank you."

"Total silence. From now on. Total fucking silence. You ever see that movie, *Fargo*? Or maybe it's called *Fargo in Space* here since you're a alien? An alien? Man, that's so sweet! I took an alien to the fucking Bone Zone in SPACE! Hitting g-spots in zero-g! Oowee!"

Seeree considered using her telekinesis to shut Baron up by ripping out his larynx, but then the sword of baklava goblin did it for her.

Baron's eyes rolled back into his skull, and he collapsed to the ground: dead, dead, deadski.

Desert World
(2-2)

Baron's eyes rolled forward into his skull and he rose from the ground: alive, alive, aliveski.

Next to him on the sand was a baklava goblin diced into little nut and pastry bits. Next to it, Seeree knelt on the ground. The lower half of her face was drenched in blood.

"Whoa, what the fart happened?" Baron rasped through his newly repaired voicebox.

"You idiot!" Seeree sobbed. "Do you have any idea how much telekinetic energy it takes to resurrect someone? I needed that for the battle against Dweem, and now were fucked!"

"Damn, sorry," Baron said. He stood up and walked over to her. "Do you need a tissue for your STEM major nose blood?"

"Yes, please," Seeree coughed. She looked up at him and smirked. "I'm glad you're okay."

"Thanks. I actually don't, um, have any tissues, though. I just thought I should ask."

"Not as glad now." Seeree scooped up a handful of sand and crammed it into her nostrils to stop the bleeding.

"Hey, to be fair," Baron said, digging himself even deeper, "I was most likely on my way to Pumphalla when you ripped me back to this Dessert Bullshit World, so thank you but also no thank you."

"It hasn't even been five minutes yet," Seeree grumbled.

"That's on you," Baron said while cramming a bit of sand into his own nose to see what it felt like. "But don't worry. I was honestly planning on bailing after I got Garindax back, but since you saved my life because you love me and my rip so much, I guess I'll help you with the 7 Pumpedly Pins stuff. You got any ideas/strategy guides to let us know where it could be in this world?"

Seeree sighed as she pointed a bloody, sandy finger at the only structure on the otherwise empty horizon—a giant pyramid with a glowing "*PIN IS IN HERE*" neon sign above a sealed door.

"Heh heh, 'pin is,'" Baron chuckled. "So good."

He scooped up Seeree because she was still weak, but also because he needed to hug something soft and warm since he was still a bit freaked out about dying and not knowing where his best buddy was.

Baron jet-booted toward the pyramid's door (his fuel refilled from early, so just chill). As he and Seeree descended upon the conical stack of sugar cubes, the door opened to reveal a pitch-black aperture filled with huge, gleaming fangs.

Desert World
(2-💀)

"Oh fart! Boss time!" Baron shouted. He blazed down to the fangs, set Seeree safely behind him, and assumed a power stance of maximum intensity. He immediately realized that he had no plan, so his stance reduced to medium intensity.

"Relax," Seeree said as she pushed past him. "These are just decorative. They're wax." She tapped on one of the stalactite teeth, which crumbled from the ceiling and crashed into one of the stalagmite teeth growing from the ground.

"Hmm. Is that technically candy?" Baron replied warily.

"Sure. They make wax fangs for Halloween, don't they?"

"Yeah, but are you supposed to actually *eat* them?"

"I don't think you're *supposed* to, but everyone knows if you do you'll have melty Dracula fangs

88

in your poop, so it's at the very least implied. Fucking don't do it and then sue me, though."

Baron and Seeree punched, chewed, and swallowed their way into the pyramid.

"It's kind of a bummer that this wasn't actually a boss," Baron said with his mouth full of soon-to-be-poop-fang. "One time, me and Garindax fought this big, perverted lip monster that had a clever pun name but also wanted to touch us."

"A perverted lip monster?" Seeree balked. "That sounds stupid. And why would it want to touch you?"

"I dunno! Because it was a frigg'n weirdo ped."

"You were a kid when you fought it?"

"No, this was like three years ago."

"So, you were an adult."

"Fine. It was a perv then. Same difference."

"…Do you *want* to be touched?"

"No way!"

"I dunno. I think you do."

"Can we just drop this?!" Baron shouted. He nervously snapped off another fang and took a bite. "Fucking gross!"

"Yeah, wax candy sucks," a sultry voice called from down the shaft. "Everyone knows that. It's why I use it for my decorations, so no one comes in here and starts eating my shit like they're fucking Hansel and Gretel in Space."

Baron and Seeree followed the sound of the voice into a large, open chamber with a bunch of sliding block puzzles that Baron was glad he didn't have to do but Seeree was bummed she didn't get to do.

In the middle in a cage was a genie babe made of red velvet cake and wearing a gold fondant belly dancer outfit covered in turmeric sprinkles. Not in a racist way, just in an exotic way.

"Help!" she called. "Get me out of here, and I'll grant you each a wish."

"We got you. But first, what were you saying about wax candy?" Baron asked. "Are you supposed to actually eat it?"

"That wasn't me," the genie replied in a panic. "It was her!"

Baron spun around and got nailed in the face with a fist of hair.

The hair retreated and flipped back to reveal another babe genie. She was made of dark chocolate and wore a black fondant belly dancer outfit covered in squid ink sprinkles. Again, not in a racist way, just in a "she's likely a bad guy because of our primordial fear of the dark" way.

"Hairllo Hansel, hairllo Gretel" she cooed. It was the same sultry voice as before. "I am Hairem Hairlotta. It's a pleasure to hairmeet you."

Baron rushed at the dark chocolate genie because he didn't want to hear any more terrible puns, but as soon as he took two steps he was blasted back onto his butt.

"Careful, Seeree!" Baron said. "She's a telekinetic STEM major, too!"

"That was me, you idiot," Seeree snarled. "Like I already told you, I can't resurrect you a second time. So, you need to sit this one out."

The dark genie babe raised her eyebrows and looked down at Baron. "You're on your zero life?" she said with a condescending smirk. "Well, then, wouldn't it be terrible if someone were to *take it* from you?"

"Yeah, prolly," Baron replied matter-of-factly.

"Hi. About to kill you here," Seeree said while holding up one hand to prepare a telekinetic death-blast, and the other to stop her nosebleed.

The genie laughed and sashayed past her toward Baron. "Do you know what they used to call orgasms during the Middle Ages in Space? *Petit mortes.* Little deaths. How many little deaths do you think you have in that zero life of yours?"

She pulled a poison ghost pepper lip gloss from her cleavage, put it on awkwardly/unevenly, and leaned down to kiss Baron on his mouth or maybe wiener.

Baron couldn't move because he was kind of turned on but also because Seeree had given him shit about wanting to be touched, so he felt like if he ran away from a babe kiss, he'd be done.

Right before Hairem's lips connected with either of Baron's heads, her hair morphed back into a fist and smashed herself in the face.

The genie's dark chocolate lips exploded open, causing the poison lining them to ooze into her bloodstream and kill her from spice intoxication.

"Told you I was about to kill you, bitch," Seeree said angrily. She stepped over the genie's corpse, giving it a couple swift kicks, then offered Baron a hand. "Why didn't you listen?"

"Because she was into me," Baron responded sadly while taking Seeree's hand. "She was willing to risk her life for the chance at just…one… kiss. What else could it be?"

"Maybe the fact that everyone always assumes the dude is a bigger threat than the girl, even when she's a STEM major and he's from Planet, where are you from? Planet DumDumTard?"

Baron didn't answer, and Seeree turned to find him already macking on the red velvet genie in the cage.

"Oh, thank you, kind sir," the genie said as he opened her cage. "My name is Shantay. You may now have your reward wish. What do you desire of me?"

"Let's see those cake jugs," Baron said without missing a beat.

She dropped her fondant harem bra, and a pair of perfectly shaped cupcake boobs flopped out.

"You moron!" Seeree shrieked from below. "You could've wished for your stupid guitar friend, or the rest of the pins, or infinity wishes! Fucking cake boobs?!"

She telekinetically ripped Baron out of the cage and then ripped the cage from the ceiling. It crashed to the ground and skewered the genie, sending curry gelato (worldly/not racist), all over the place.

"I don't need to wish for Garindax, babe," Baron said coolly as he jet-booted to the ground. "Because he's chilling right over there in that sarcophagus guitar case. Hey, P.S., you killed her before cashing in your reward wish, so now who's from Planet DumDumTard?"

"FUCK!" Seeree screamed. She rushed over and tried to reshape Shantay, but now the cake was too wet from the gelato and there was some sand mixed into it, so it was ruined/gross.

While Seeree freaked out and dealt with another nosebleed, Baron strode over to the sarcophagus guitar case that had emerged after he single-handily defeated the boss.

As he removed the sarcophagus lid, he noticed that it wasn't a guitar case at all, but a ukulele case. Inside it was, appropriately, a tiny ukulele being held, inappropriately, by a tiny mushroom alien wearing a penis-shaped turban.

"Whoa, Spike Vegelta!?" Baron shouted in surprise. "What are you doing here?"

"I'm not Spike Vegelta," the mushroom alien replied. "That was my brother. I'm Spike Vagelta. 'Tis a pleasure."

"I gotta know, Spike. Where's Garindax?"

"Try Water World," he responded wisely. "Sometimes, Desert World contains a lot of water levels, but other times Water World is entirely separate. This is one of those times."

"Which times?"

"The latter one."

"Ladder..."

"The separate one," Seeree jumped in.

"Got it," Baron nodded. "Next question. What's under the hat?"

"You already know what's under—" Seeree started.

"Sorry," Spike interrupted with his eyes closed and his nose in the air. "It's top secret."

"C'mon, tell us," Baron pleaded.

"Okay. I'll tell you," Spike said. "It's…"

Baron held his breath.

"…a top seeks."

"Oh my fuck," Seeree snapped *figuratively*, before she snapped *literally* Spike Vagelta's neck.

His corpse clattered to the ground, sending his turban flying off and a pin shaped like a cactus with a hilt rolling across the sand.

"Pick that shit up," she sternly ordered Baron. "And meet me at the car." She strolled out of the pyramid, leaving Baron to figure out if she wanted him to pick up the corpse, the turban, or the pin.

It took over an hour for him to decide incorrectly.

Water World
(3-1)

"Okay, Water World," Seeree said determinedly as she landed her hovercar on a raw sugar beach. "This should be pretty straightforward. We found the pin in the sand in the last world, so this time it's gotta be in the ocean. Let's jump in and swim around until we find it."

Baron didn't say anything.

"Oh yeah," Seeree realized. She telekinetically unglued Baron's jaw.

"—*uuuuuuck!*" Baron exhaled. "Not cool! You know I have a deviated septum and can't breathe through my nose that well."

"But you also wouldn't shut the fuck up about the 'top seeks' of Spot Bahelta."

"It was Spike Vagelta, and/or Spike Vegelta, and I just wanted to know how you knew what was under their hats!"

"I already explained that," Seeree snapped. "It's a stupid pun. The only thing that's unexplained is why you're so obsessed with the fucking things. Between your numerous encounters with perv monsters, ped monsters, and now the penis-hat fixation, I'm beginning to think you're a little freaky-deaky. What's next? Am I going to find out you have mom issues?"

"Coming from someone who slept with their maybe-dad," Baron snapped back, or clapped back, or whatever the shit. "You didn't have any problems with that!"

"Yeah, and neither did you."

"Exactly. So, now do you believe me?"

"Believe you what?!" Seeree laughed. "That you're more intrigued by the *mystery* of the mushroom aliens' penis hats than the fact that they're shaped like penises?"

"Yes! Wait, no."

"I'll believe whatever ends this conversation."

"So, friends/lovers/stepdad-and-stepdaughter again?"

"Yes/no/oh-fuck-I-guess-we-technically-are, huh?"

"Yep. It's kind of hot, if you think about it. Maybe making you rethink your second slash?"

"Nope, only the first one," Seeree replied. "And, see, I told you that you were freaky-deaky. Now shut your own mouth for a bit so I don't have to waste telekinetic ammo re-gluing it. I need some food that's not candy, so I'm going to catch us some fish tendies. And then we're going swimming without waiting 30 minutes."

"Can you please rethink your second slash?" Baron asked.

"No way. I don't think I like dudes *at all* after hanging out with you. My future girlfriend thanks you because I'm probably going to be really good at doing stuff. And on that note, check this shit out."

Seeree stared into the cobalt ocean and narrowed her eyes. As soon as her nose dropped a single blood flake, she raised a hand and yanked a giant, two-pronged fish tendie tail from the sea.

"Jackpot," she said with a smile that still had the blood flake chilling on it.

She pulled harder, and from out of the ocean and onto the island popped a mermaid alien who was half tendie, half babe. Both halves looked super hot: the tendie half temperature-wise, and the babe half sexy-wise.

But the babe side also looked super *pissed*, so Baron and Seeree knew they were frigg'n in for it.

Water World (3-2)

"Hey, bitch, why'd you pull me out of the water?" the mermaid demanded while clacking her super long fingernails together. "I was actually having a pretty good day before that."

"Uh…" Seeree hesitated.

"Because we were going to eat you," Baron whatever is the opposite of hesitated.

"Oh, honey," the mermaid said while looking Baron up and down. "All you needed to do was ask me nicely."

Baron started to pop a bone, but then the mermaid fish-flopped over to him, so it kind of went away.

"Don't bother," Seeree said dismissively. "He's only interested in aliens with penis hats."

"Not true!" Baron remarked. "I mean, not that there's anything wrong with that."

"Of course not, sugar," the mermaid said seductively. She did another fish-flop and pressed herself against Baron. "As a matter of fact, I like my victims a little freaky-deaky."

Baron re-popped a bone, but in doing so it crinkled against the mermaid's fried fish half, so it kind of went away again. Plus, he realized that she had said "victims."

"Hey, what do you mean by—" Baron started.

"Shh," she whispered with tartar sauce breath. She placed one long fingernail over Baron's lips, and with her other hand reached slowly into his pocket. As soon as he started to re-re-pop a bone, she yanked her hand out without touching anything beginning with 'p' other than 'pins,' so it re-re-went-went away.

"Baron, stop her!" Seeree yelled. "She stole our Worlds 1 and 2 pins!"

Unfortunately, Baron was incapable of doing anything at the moment because of crippling blue balls.

The mermaid fish-flopped frantically back toward the ocean. Seeree fired a telekinetic blast at her but missed, instead obliterating a banana-flavored taffy seagull that had a stupid joke printed on its belly.

"Heh heh, thanks for the pins," the mermaid called over her bare shoulder. "They'll make great ear or maybe nipple rings. I haven't decided yet and need to talk to my boyfriend about it first."

"Aw man, *boyfriend?*" Baron grumbled.

"Yeah," the mermaid replied. "He's kind of overprotective and thinks that if I get my nipples pierced it means I'm like, loose. But the hypocritical thing is he thinks it's *hot*, too. Besides, he has his nipples pierced, so does that mean *he's* loose?"

"Yes," Seeree answered bluntly.

She fired another telekinetic blast, but the sun caught her eye. The blast missed and hit a coconut, causing it explode and shower candied coconut shreds onto the beach.

"I've seen how he flirts with this cashier at Target in Space," the mermaid continued, undeterred. "Every time we go, he asks her how to use the new Target in Space Circle membership thing, and then when she answers, he's all like, 'Oh, that's dope.' But it's not dope. Nothing about saving 1% or flirting with stupid skanks is dope. We had a big fight about it. Anyway, catch you on the *flip!*"

She flipped into the ocean and booked it.

"C'mon, we gotta go after her!" Seeree yelled as she not-even-telekinetically pushed Baron to the sand, jumped on his back, and kicked his boots together to transform him into a jet-powered and quickly drowning surfboard.

Water World
(3-💀)

Seeree blasted across the water with her Baron-board, making sure to kickflip every now and then so he could breathe, but also so she could look cool.

"Slow down, bish!" she yelled at the mermaid.

"No, way!" the mermaid retorted.

"Dammit, Baron, speed your boots up!" Seeree shouted while leaning over and twisting Baron's earlobe super hard.

Baron winced and stared down at the ocean floor and all of the fish looking sad at him.

I wish I was back in my apartment playing VR games with Garindax, he thought. *And I especially wish I didn't have to be a surfboard.*

Fortunately, he didn't have to be for much longer, as the mermaid came to an abrupt stop when she reached a part of the ocean that had a giant "5 FEET" sign floating on top of it.

"Time out!" the aquatic tendie princess cried. "We can't go into the deep end without a life guard on duty. By the way, my name is Chestly in case you're tired of calling me 'mermaid.'"

But Seeree didn't hear her since she was too busy yelling at Baron. She slammed into Chestly, boobs first because both of their boobs (four boobs total) were sticking out farther than their other body parts. They immediately started fighting over the pins, churning the water and making their boobs all soapy.

It was almost enough to make the entire bullshit trip worth it, and Baron began to pinch tips (in slow motion since he was underwater). On the tenth pinch, he remembered all of the fish below him, so he stopped and acted like he had just been adjusting his swimsuit the whole time. But it was too late: an entire school (as in a group, not fish kids) saw everything. They tried not to look, but they did and felt super spicy/guilty about it.

While Baron and the fish wrestled with their weird feelings, Seeree and Chestly kept wrestling with each other over the pins. The water popped and fizzed, causing the boob soap to lather and the pins to become mega slippery.

"Baron, the pins!" Seeree yelled as they flew from Chestly's hands up into the light blue sky, and then down into the dark blue ocean.

Baron dove after the gleaming jewels, making sure to avoid eye contact with the school of fish as he descended. He scooped the pins up from the sandy bottom and turned around to swim back up, but in doing so found himself face to fin with a Swedish fish who handed him a note that read, "*Do you like me? Yes/No/Maybe*"

After circling "Maybe," which Baron thought was a nice way of letting the fish down but really just caused it to turn even redder and believe it was now in a meaningful relationship, Baron swam back to the surface.

"Did you get them?! Give them to me!" Seeree demanded as soon as he reemerged.

"No, give them to me!" Chestly pleaded. "I'll give you anything you want: beejay, gilljay, you name it! Whatever that Swedish fish just offered you will seem like a peck on the peen when I'm finished with you! Trust me, my boyfriend is right: I'm super loose!"

"Okay, but give me the jays *first*," Baron replied.

"Oh my fuck, he doesn't even have them," Seeree groaned.

"Well, I did have them for a bit," Baron started, "but then I got scared/pumped because I saw—"

Suddenly, a gigantic gummy shark erupted through the frothy waves of boob soap. It flipped, opened its mouth, and enveloped the mermaid whole.

"—a giant gummy shark."

"FUCK!" Seeree shouted.

The gummy shark busted back up through the swell and raised its shades.

"Syrup?" it burped. A pierced mermaid nip fell into the ocean.

"Oh, man! This dude rules!" Baron cheered.

Seeree didn't respond because she was underwater, searching for the pins and also trying not to get eaten.

"Thanks, man," the shark said radly. "And thanks for not being scared of me. I don't know what everyone's problem is. Like, I love that your mom just insta-bailed as soon as I showed up."

"No way, man," Baron reassured the shark while not revealing that he had only a few seconds ago booked it from him, and that Seeree wasn't his mom, but technically his stepdaughter.

"So, what are y'all getting into?" The shark asked. "Just ocean chilling?"

"Yeah, man," Baron replied. "It's a good day for it. The sun is out and stuff." He had become really good at socializing since he started playing online games with chat functionality.

"Totally. That's a great point. I think it's time to go *Shade Mode On.*" The shark re-lowered his shades. "Anyway, I'm Game Shark. I think that's safe to tell you. It would've been a problem at one point, but now I don't think anyone cares. Just in case, I'm Parody Game Shark."

"That's dope," Baron said because he thought it had sounded cool when Chestly said it.

"Haha, I like your style, dude. You want a frigg'n wish?"

"Sure. Thanks, mon," Baron said in a cool Jamaican accent. "And do you want to see me do Liu Kang's bicycle kick? It's really easy in water."

"Haha oh shit. Now you're up to *three* wishes."

Seeree found and snagged the pins from the ocean floor right before it transformed into Ghoul-Aid. *Ohmyfuck,* she cursed while turning and churning through the sugary (not bullshit artificial sweetener), purple (not bullshit blue) liquid.

As she crested the surface, her fears were confirmed upon finding Baron wearing his brand-new shades with hologram ghosts from The Real Ghostbusters printed on the lenses.

"One more wish, mahdu," Game Shark said with a grin.

"Baron, stop!" Seeree said.

But it was too late. Game Shark lowered his shades and winked.

A chicken banh mi materialized in each of Baron's hands.

"You moron!" Seeree shouted. She was about to kill him and the gummy shark, but then she recalled her hastiness with the genie.

"Okay, so now it's my turn, right?" she asked calmly but through clenched teeth. "I get a wish, or two, or however many this motherfucker just wasted. Right, Mr. Nice Gummy Shark Monster?"

"No, way, bia-bia," Game Shark scoffed. "You ran away from me because you were scared/sharksist, so I don't owe you shit. Plus, you shouldn't call your kid a 'motherfucker.' It makes you sound kind of freaky-deaky."

"AAARGH!" Seeree yelled. She telekinetically ripped off Game Shark's shades, forcing him to go *Shade Mode Off* and lowering his coolness by a bunch. Then she telekinetically flipped the shades and rammed them back into his eye sockets, technically reactivating Shade Mode but also killing him, so it was a net loss.

She then swirled the water and flushed Game Shark to the briny deep, where those fish with lightbulbs on their heads rubbed their lightbulbs all over his body. His last thoughts were of hope that maybe the fish were trying to heal him with their lightbulb power, but then of despair as he realized they were just being gross.

"You," Seeree growled while slowly bringing the water around her and Baron to a boil.

"Are you pissing?" Baron asked disgustedly. "Because, uh, rude."

Seeree raised the temperature and continued growling. "You could've wished for the rest of the pins. Or to kill Dweem so we wouldn't even need them. Or even to get your stupid guitar back. But you wasted them on, what? A Ghoul-Aid ocean?"

"A *parody* Ghoul-Aid ocean, just in case. Maybe 'Ghoul-Ade,' spelled—"

"And stupid little kid shades."

"No, baller RGB hologram shades."

"And now this. A chicken fucking sandwich."

"*Two* chicken *banh mi* sandwiches. One for me and one for you. That was to show you that I'm growing as an individual and not being, uh, selfless."

"...Selfish."

"Shellfish."

Seeree used every STEM power in her arsenal to raise the water around Baron to 211 degrees Fahrenheit, and just as she was about to give it that last, fatal degree, everything went black.

Chocolate World (4-1)

"Wake up, mama!" a tiny voice called.

Seeree's eyes blinked opened. Everything was still black, but beginning to fade to a dark brown. She sat up and realized that she was riding the jet-powered Baron-board again, but this time she was rocketing through the air.

In a panic, she reached down and clung voraciously to one of his cheeks (butt, not face). Clinging voraciously to his other cheek was a mushroom alien wearing a starfish-shaped hat.

"Starfish!" Baron called from the underside of his butt. "I meant to say starfish, not shellfish. As in, 'Watch out for the flying starfish.' Sorry about that!"

"And *I'm* sorry I got too pumped and did that cannonball into the ocean," the mushroom alien said using the tiny voice from before. "I didn't mean to knock you out."

"Wha…what the fuck is going on?" Seeree gasped. "Aren't you Spike…Vegelta? Or was it Spike Vagelta?"

"No, those guys are jerks. I'm Sam Vehelta."

"Sam? But then where is the pin? It can't be in your hat. It's starfish-shaped."

"Look closer," Sam said as he wiggled over.

Seeree's eyes focused and noticed the phallic detail on each of the starfish's five points.

"The pin is in here," Sam said excitedly, now way too close. He tipped his hat and the third pin fell into Seeree's cleavage.

"Oops! Butter fingers, butter fingers," he laughed nervously while using his free hand to chase after the pin.

"Hey, hands off, creep!" Seeree shouted while using her free hand to bat Sam away.

"Sorry!" Sam apologized. "I was trying to help you by giving you the pin for free. I was only trying to be nice."

"It's fine, but just chill. You are very nice. Thank you for the pin."

Seeree looked down and fished out the pin from between her boobs, causing them to squish and squelch like high-end stress balls that you can only order from a magazine on an airplane.

When she finally found it (along with a bonus Goldfish cracker), she looked up and also found that Sam was now an inch from her face.

"Do you like to kiss?" he whispered with warm milk-and-broccoli breath.

Seeree telekinetically repelled him like a magnet repels another magnet when it's facing a certain way, but not the other way because then they hang out.

"Seeree, what the fart?!" Baron yelled as he saw his new friend hurtling toward the brown terrain below. He descended after Sam, but it was too late. The mushroom alien nailed a rocky peak and splattered into a pool of maraschino slime.

"He tried to kiss me!" Seeree explained as Baron landed because now he was bummed out and needed to walk around for a bit.

"You owed him that much!" he replied. "Complete with tongue biting and lip sucking!"

"I think you mean—"

"Sam saved your life after you passed out and sank into the ocean. I obviously couldn't go after you because I was holding the chicken banh mis, which I couldn't get wet in case Sam saved you, which he *did*. His starfish hat worked like a propeller and everything. It ruled!"

"Well, none of that matters because he's dead, and we have the pin," Seeree replied uncaringly. "It's shaped like a shark tooth with a hilt, in case you're keeping track of these things."

"Not really. But the hilt is on the bottom of the shark tooth?"

"Obviously. Man, you need a lot of hand-holding. Where are we, by the way?"

"Um, Chocolate World," Baron said warily.

"*Chocolate World?*" Seeree asked more warily.

"Yep…" Baron responded most warily.

"Sounds…potentially problematic," Seeree said ultimost warily.

"Yeah, I actually told Sam 'no way' at first, but he assured me this is definitely the next stop for pins/Garindaxes."

"Okay, let's start questing then. Hey, where's my chicken banh mi?"

"I think I see part of it over there in Sam's ripped-open stomach."

Chocolate World (4-2)

Chocolate World wasn't problematic—it was *bad as fart*.

Dark chocolate ghosts and castles were everywhere, and spooky music blasted from milk chocolate harpsichords chilling next to white chocolate gravestones filled with peanut butter, chocolate chips, and/or rice krispies.

"Ho hoo! This rules!" Baron yelled as he tore down a road of M&M cobblestones that crunched satisfyingly underfoot.

He laughed at how worried he had been when Sam Vehelta told him where they were going, and how Sam had picked up on his apprehension, so he recommended they distract themselves by taking turns kissing Seeree while she was still unconscious. Just for practice, so if she wanted to kiss when she woke up, they'd be better at it.

And it worked out beautifully!

Had Baron not agreed to take turns kissing unconscious Seeree, he might've ended up giving into his fear and telling Sam they should go somewhere else because he "wasn't really into" Chocolate World, or maybe that he "was looking for something better" than Chocolate World.

Both of those excuses had their own potentially problematic interpretations, so Baron would've been danged if he did, and danged if he didn't. Either way, he would've been danged. Royally fucking danged.

But since he had instead distracted himself from his anxieties by kissing, everything worked out fine. Now he was having a cool adventure, and he got more kissing practice in to boot. There was probably a very important lesson there, but Baron was too pumped to think about it any longer.

"How sweet it is!" he cheered as he diverted from the main road and into a forest of looming cocoa trees that were ominously dripping caramel sap onto the chocolate-coated marshmallow path below.

"Baron, chill the fuck out!" Seeree called after him. "You're getting too pumped!"

She tried to keep up, but at some point Baron activated his jet boots, so the only trace of him was a trail of toasted marshmallow and a tiny dot that was indistinguishable from the chocolate chips on the horizon.

"Motherfucker…" she grumbled as one of her feet became stuck in the marshmallow sludge. She pulled it out, causing her shoe to get sucked into the sticky mire.

She bent down and attempted to fish it out, which exposed her early 2000s whale-tail thong. Suddenly, something pressed up against her backside and whispered, "Hey, girl scout…you got any *cookies?* PS do you like to kiss?"

Chocolate World
(4-💀)

Seeree turned to find herself face-to-pinched-tip with a giant, white chocolate ghost monster. It had candy corn teeth, red hot eyes, licorice whiskers, pretzel-stick hands, and a peanut-butter pumpkin crown on top of its hollow head.

"Trick or treat, mama," the ghost king wheezed with breath that smelled like rotten pumpkin guts. "I'm King Priapus, final boss of this world. And today's your lucky day. I'm going to let you be my queen."

Seeree didn't say shit or even use her telekinetic powers—she just headbutted the fuck out King Priapus right in the pinched tip.

With a howl, his red hot eyes turned to sour blue razz Warheads, his licorice whiskers curled, and the tip he had been pinching crumbled into little crumbles.

"You bitch! How dare you reject the crown and my tip?" he shouted. "You stupid, lascivious broads are all the same. You bend over, exposing bottom of cheek and top of thong while thrusting your arm into sticky white goo, and then you act like you don't want it!"

"Want *what?!* I was just trying to get my shoe!" Seeree yelled back.

"Yeah, well now you're going to get *this!*"

From the depths of King Priapus' cavernous tip void, a slightly smaller tip emerged.

He commenced to pinching.

"And you stupid, rapacious creeps are all the same," Seeree chuckled.

She headbutted the tip again and heard something crack, but when she pulled her head back the tip remained and was now surrounded by stars. At the tip of the tip, red liquid oozed onto the ground.

Seeree put her hand to her throbbing forehead and pulled back a handful of blood.

"Heh heh heh," King Priapus laughed as he moved his pinching fingers to his bulbous nose. "What do we have here?" he asked with a sniff. "Grenadine for my chocolate treats?"

Seeree reeled.

King Priapus popped the bloody finger into his mouth. "Gross," he muttered with a smile.

He removed his hand and hovered closer. "And now, my dear, it's your turn to…take the taste."

Seeree shot a telekinetic blast, but since she was still kind of fucked up it missed and hit a fudge tree branch. A cotton candy moth fluttered out and gave her a concerned look, like it knew the shit it was seeing wasn't cool.

"Tell me, Mr. Moth," the ghost king wheezed. He wrapped his filthy pretzelled hands around Seeree's pounding head. "How many licks does it take to get to the center of a Tipsy Pop? A one…a two-hoo…a—"

Before he got to three or did anything *actually* gross (don't worry), brown liquid sprayed across King Priapus' tip.

The liquid sizzled, and each of the tip's 100 jawbreaker layers quickly but painfully melted away until it exposed the bubblegum center, which slowly but even more painfully expanded into a giant balloon and popped.

Gum shot all over King Priapus' own face at the very same time the GhostWorldoogle map car was driving by to take pictures of the street.

"*NOOO!*" King Priapus roared. "My tips! My precious tips!"

His hollow body imploded and then exploded across the marshmallow ground, where a bunch of chocolate-covered ants immediately devoured everything except his pretzel hand because it had touched tip.

Seeree pulled herself to her feet with a groan.

"Hey, where's your shoe?" a familiar voice asked.

She turned around and saw Baron riding atop a 100% cacao dragon. On one side of him sat a mushroom alien wearing a fez, and on the other side sat an empty paper cup.

"They have the ballerest hot chocolate here," Baron said. "I brought you one. Well, I *brought* you one—meaning, like, I tried—but then I spilled it on that ghost's...what the fuck was that? Was that his wiener? Were you doing stuff with him? I mean, it's cool if we're not exclusive since we didn't really talk about it, but *I* just had the opportunity to do stuff with a pan dulce princess, and I didn't because I thought that maybe you and I were. But then I found our boy here, um—"

"Sam Vahelta," the mushroom alien said with a polite bow.

"See, how frigg'n dope is this place?" Baron continued. "And, look, he's just wearing a fez, not a penis hat, or a fez with little penis tassels, or anything stupid. Plus, he straight-up said we could have this world's pin without even fighting any boss monsters. It looks like a classic haunted house with a hilt. So, boom! Chocolate World is finished, you got hot chocolate delivery, I didn't cheat on you with Princesa de Las Tetas, and a fez-wearing alien is handing us the pin for free. See? No nonsense this time! Just normal stuff and pump. Just normal and pump from now on. Don't worry, mama. Just normal and pump from now on."

Seeree doubled over as a shock of pain coursed through her skull. She slammed her eyes shut, and because her forehead hadn't stopped bleeding from earlier, all she saw was red.

Ice World
(5-1)

Seeree hadn't said a word. Baron and Sam hadn't stopped talking.

"So, mufugging Ice World is next?!" Baron said excitedly as he and Sam Vahelta roughhoused on a dragon wing the size of a football field.

"You know it!" Sam replied before chomping into Baron's arm.

"Ouch!" Baron shouted. He pinched Sam's neck scruff to let him know he was playing too hard.

"Sorry," Sam responded. "I was the runt of the litter, so my alien mushroom siblings never took the time to teach me how to wrestle properly."

"It's okay," Baron said. "I'm teaching you now, so that makes us brothers in battle/life forever."

"Whoa…" Sam replied as that intense realization sank in.

"Back to Ice World," Baron continued while tackling Sam. "Is it a fucking bullshit ice world where everything is just slippery but otherwise it's the same as grass world, or is it like a badass ice world where everything is Christmassy and there are nutso lights and present pickups?"

Sam kicked out of the tackle and started to bark because he was getting too pumped. When he finally calmed down, he nodded toward the edge of the dragon's wing and said, "Dude, you tell me."

Baron's eyes grew in pumpticipation, and he looked over the dragon's wing just as Christmas lights were coming into focus in the distance. Beyond them, he heard jingle bells.

"*Fuck yeah!*" he yelled. "You rule, Sam Vehelta, even if you and your fellow mushroom alien buddies are false pumps for Garindax. But, hey, isn't this the, uh, next to last world? Does that mean Garindax will be there for sure? I need him to fight the final boss, and I don't want to do a bunch of bullshit back-tracking. But now we have five pins, so doesn't that make this the, um, pentultermant world? I mean, peppermint world? Is that why it's Ice World, acause it's Peppermint World?"

Seeree lost it. She telekinetically snapped the dragon's neck, sending it and everyone careening into a powdered sugar snowbank.

Baron and Sam dug themselves out and looked up at her in terror.

"We only have *four* pins," she snarled, "and we need *seven*. That doesn't make this the next to last world, which would be the *penultimate* world, not the fucking peppermint world. And his name is Sam *Vahelta*, not Vehelta. Like Spike Vegelta and Vagelta. There must be a pattern there, but I haven't been able to figure it out yet. Or maybe there isn't a pattern, and it's just nonsense for nonsense sake. I don't know. More importantly, I don't care. I don't care about you aliens."

"You aliens?" Baron repeated defensively. "Did you hear that, Sam? She said 'you aliens.'"

"Who the hell is *us aliens?*" Sam demanded. He stood up and began growling.

A drop of blood fell from Seeree's nose, and it hit the powdered sugar snow in perfect unison with Sam Vahelta's twisted, lifeless body.

Baron scurried backward, kicking his jetboots together and melting the snow around his feet into what looked like a puddle of piss.

"You…you care about me, though, don't you?" Baron asked nervously.

"No," Seeree responded while wiping her nose and turning toward Ice World.

"I need you."

Ice World
(5-2)

Baron and Seeree trekked across the powdered sugar, but fortunately not that cold, tundra.

Eventually/literally, they stumbled upon a large gumdrop polar bear.

"Oh, dang, this must be the boss," Baron whispered. "I think he's asleep."

"How can you tell?" Seeree asked.

"Because he's snoring."

"No, you moron. How can you tell that he's the boss?"

"Look at this giant fuck. He's a frigg'n bear. What, do you think the boss is going to be this little bishass?" Baron pointed to a little Dutch mint boy with social anxiety and pajamas with the butt-flap *un*buttoned.

"You're right," Seeree acknowledged. "Alright, let's get the pin. I'm still low on energy from killing Sam, so we'll have to do this the fun way."

Without even discussing strategy, they kicked the polar bear in the gumdrops at the exact same time: Baron kicking the right and Seeree kicking the left, which for some reason was slightly smaller than the right.

They gasped and looked at each other.

Both had dump feeling, but in a spicy/love way. They wanted nothing more than to reach out and hold the other's hand, but they hesitated because they weren't sure if the other would be down. And then the bear shot out of the snow with a pained roar, so it was too late.

"OWIE!" he yelled. "Hey, what's the big ideal?" The polar bear had a super dumb voice and said "ideal," which even Baron knew was wrong, so he and Seeree immediately realized that this dude couldn't be the final boss.

"Sorry to bust your balls," Seeree apologized. "We were hoping you were the boss of this world so we could get the pin and get out of here."

"Do oo mean the sparkle-sparkle?" the polar bear asked dreamily.

Baron and Seeree both cringed at how stupid and baby he sounded. Even if he had learning disabilities, which they knew he couldn't help, it was simply too much when coupled with the fact that he was a big bear made of gumdrops, even though he couldn't help that, either.

But they could imagine the idiot 30-year-olds who would clamor over a plush version of him; the 30-year-olds who would end up fucking that plush in their dark childhood bedrooms that reeked of Bagel Bites; and the 30-year-olds who would cosplay as it while getting fucked in the bathroom of a Crowne Plaza that's hosting the convention where adults share sodas, stinks, and sexually transmitted infections.

"Excoose me," the bear said. "Do oo mean the sparkle-sparkle?"

Baron and Seeree snapped out of their trance. "Unfortunately, probably," she sighed. "It looks like these."

She showed the bear the other pins.

"Them's sparkle-sparkles!" he said excitedly. "Bohsoo Bear know where there is anuhdoo sparkle-sparkle! Bohsoo Bear will take oo there!"

"Ugh, this fuckin' guy," Seeree said in a disgusted Jersey accent.

Baron started to pop a bone, and he pinched himself (on the leg, not tip) as punishment for not grabbing her hand earlier.

"Yeah, he definitely sucks," Baron responded. "But maybe we should give him a break because he might be r-worded and/or able to give us the pin. Let's not kill him until we know for sure. And who knows? Maybe we'll learn about his life and challenges, which will make us feel better about our own lives because we're not him, but also because we helped him by not killing him. Either way, we come out great."

Seeree was so impressed by Baron's social skills/prowess that she pinched herself (on the leg, not tip [which a woman *does* have, but it's almost impossible to pinch unless they're in a bathtub]) as punishment for not grabbing his hand earlier.

Bohsoo Bear dug into the powdered sugar snowbank to reveal an entrance to a black/blue tunnel.

"Oo race Bohsoo Bear!" he said. "Oo win, and Bohsoo Bear will take oo to Queen Areola!"

"Queen Areola?" Seeree asked.

"Queen Areola!" Baron yelled as he leapt after the stupid gumdrop bear and the prospect of briefly interacting with another babe in this stupid world in this stupid galaxy.

"But if oo loose…" Bohsoo Bear called back. "Bohsoo Bear will give oo something *horrible*."

"Yeesh, that's a little ominous," Seeree said as she dropped into the tunnel.

Ice World
(5-💀)

Baron and Seeree slip-sledded away after the polar bear while obnoxious horn music blasted in the background.

They busted around corners and over hills, and right when it looked like they were going to lose, Seeree used telekinesis to grab one of the blue sugarplum beetles that was chilling on the ceiling and lob it at Boshoo Bear.

The shell crashed into the bear's skull, shattering and sending spiked shrapnel through his eyeballs, brainballs, tongueballs, noseballs, and earballs. His head looked like it had gone through a blender. The slug-slime trail of blood made his body spin and slow down, though, allowing Baron and Seeree to slide right past it and onto the checkerboard finish platform, where Bohsoo Bear's wife was waiting with a nice blueberry pie and sobbing hysterically.

"We did it!" Baron cheered while grabbing the pie.

"Yeah," Seeree said, "but now we have to find the queen ourselves."

They proceeded off the finish platform and into the next room. Despite everything leading up to that point being pretty Christmassy, Baron and Seeree now found themselves in a dark, secular, almost sci-fi-looking cave.

Suddenly, a gigantic cookie dough snake slithered out of a corridor.

"Welcome to my ssnake dungeon!" he yelled. "My name iss Karmax, the bosss of Ice World! And there'ss no need for your introductionss, ass I know who you are. You're both fuck-bombed!"

"Wait, what the shit?" Baron asked. "A snake monster? Where is Queen Ariedonda?"

"Areola," Seeree corrected.

"Oh, damn, yeah, now *mega* where is she?" Baron demanded. "And what was that other thing you just said about 'ass'? Is there an ass queen somewhere, too?"

"Queen Cheekss, yess," the snake hissed. "SSisster of Queen Areola. Both were ssupposed to be the bosssess of thiss world."

"Oh my fuck, I hate that extra 's' thing so much," Seeree griped. "Can you just, like, be normal for one second? It's been a long day."

"Oh, okay, sure," the snake replied in a normal accountant voice. "That's actually as much of a relief to me as it is to you. I don't like adding s's to everything, but Tourism is really on my asss. Ass. Sorry. It's hard to turn off."

"It's all good," Seeree said with a smile. She was starting to dig Karmax.

Baron picked up on this and also knew that he could never compare to a snake monster's girth, so he began to get insecure. "Hey, so who's actually the boss of this world," he said, "because we really just need the pin so we can get moving. Seeree here is pregnant and on her period."

"What the fucking shit?" Seeree yelled.

"Oh yuck," Karmax said. "Anyway, like I was saying, Queens Areola and Cheeks were supposed to be the bosses of this world. Queen Areola is a gumdrop ice queen. Crazy rack, magical powers, exploding with pins and pump. Hundo nipping because her igloo is so cold. Queen Cheeks is okay. I think she wears white fur or something? Has kind of an accent? I dunno. Queen Areola is where it's at."

"Dang…" Baron said as his imagination and ping-pong went wild.

Seeree no longer dug Karmax.

"But, check it out, the devs fucked up and ran out of outer space," he continued, "so they had to use me as a boss instead. I was supposed to be the boss of Cave World, but that had to be cut to save space, too."

"What kind of shit decision is that?" Seeree snapped. "Why not just use Queens Prozzie and Harriet as the bosses of Ice World as intended, and then cut out ALL of Cave World—including you?"

"Yeah, even I can tell that's dumb," Baron said.

"Hey, man, you'd be surprised," Karmax replied. "Almost the same thing happened in the *Battletoads* arcade game. Look it up in case you hadn't already made that connection. I realize it's a deep cut. There weren't boob and butt queens, but a snake boss did replace what was supposed to be a Christmas boss in a Christmas level. And, now that I think about it, the Dark Queen is kind of a boob *and* a butt queen. Damn, she's fine. Anyway, the devs' fuck-up works for me because now I get to gobble you up. After all, I am a bigass snake."

He dove at Baron, who dove out of the way just slightly better. Karmax's stale sugar fangs pierced and became stuck in the soft ground, which was also made of cookie dough because why the fuck not.

"Baron, give me one of your boots," Seeree said.

Baron looked down and tried to decide which one to give her, the right or left, but after three minutes of deliberation she leaned down and yanked a boot off without even giving Baron the chance to explain his thought process, which was pretty rude. She activated the boot's jet thruster and began telekinetically spinning it, so it became a crazy buzzsaw of blue flames.

"Time'ss up, Ssnake Boy," she said while holding the flame up to her face.

"Oof," Baron groaned.

"Yeah, fucking cringe," Karmax said while still stuck in the ground and about to be murdered.

Seeree ignored both of them and sliced off the sugar cookie snake alien's head.

It flew into the air, spritzing icing all over the place. As the icing rained down, she continued slicing off circles of his body, which instantly cauterized into cookies baked to MF perfection.

Baron was happily chomping into his third cookie when he noticed a guitar neck sticking out of Karmax's gaping neck hole.

It was Garindax's guitar neck. And it wasn't moving.

Jungle World (6-1)

It wasn't actually Garindax.

It was a mushroom alien named Spot Velhalga, which sucked, but what blew (as in the opposite of sucked, not as in bad) was that he at least gave up the pin without a fight. It was shaped like a Christmas tree with a hilt, or a menorah with a hilt, or a Kwanzaa with a hilt, or whatever pumps your boat. His hat shared the same shape and featured some subtle element that was playfully phallic while not being blasphemous.

"Alright, Spot Velhalga," Baron said while fiddling with the inoffensive pin, "where's the next pin?" He looked over nervously at Seeree and tried, "The…pinultimate one."

"Close," Seeree said while snatching the pin from Baron's hand and putting it on her jacket. "But it's 'penultimate.' With an 'e.' You said 'i.'"

"How can you tell the difference?" Baron balked. "Asides, maybe I meant it as a clever pun."

"*Besides*. And whatever you say, penhead."

"Can y'all two stop fighting?!" Spot yelled angrily. "Damn. You're worse than my parents. Five minutes of your bickering, and I already feel like punching drywall and gauging my ears."

"Drywall can be fixed," Seeree chastised, "but if you gauge your ears, you'll immediately become and spend the rest of your days a chain-smoking sous chef with a too-old Toyota Supra and a too-young girlfriend. Don't do it."

"But do do tell us where the next p*i*n is," Baron said. "P.S., fucking doo doo."

"Fine, if it'll shut you both up," Spot said like an angsty teen. "We need to go to Jungle World."

"Jungle World?" Baron asked incredulously. "I'll set a course. But is it just going to be the same as Grass World, only with slightly stronger and palette-swapped enemies?"

"No…" Seeree whispered. "I've heard tales about Jungle World. Rumors, I hope. But they all say one thing: it's *way* worse than Grass World."

"Really? Oh, balls," Spot sighed. "Had I known that, I would've stayed back in that giant snake."

"Come to think of it, Spot," Seeree said while narrowing her eyes at the mushroom alien, "why *are* you following us? I don't recall either of us inviting or throwing a Pokéball at you."

"Well," Spot explained, "my therapist told me I was too codependent, most likely because my parents sucked, so I latch onto anyone who's half-stable. She said I should be more independent and self-sufficient. So, I took up shop in a snake alien. It actually wasn't so bad. I had a nice TV and couch setup. Even a little hot tub. But then I started to become codependent on the snake. So, when you came along and sliced my home to bits, it seemed like as good as any opportunity to move on. Honestly, though, now that I'm back in the world and listening to you fight and fart, I kind of just want to fuck off back to my snake. Maybe there's another one here that I can live in. Is that what makes Jungle World so dangerous? Snakes?"

"Shut up!" Seeree hissed. "That's not what makes this place dangerous."

The bushes rustled all around them.

"Ooh," a warbly voice cooed. "I think I hear a couple of boisterous young scouts whomst have lost their way."

"...It's PP men."

"What's that?" Baron said way too loudly. "Tropical pp suckers? I remember those from Monsteropolis. They sucked fucking pp. Oooh, is that why—"

"No. These guys make tropical pp suckers look like raspberry tt sippers," Seeree interrupted using the perfect volume given the situation. "I'm talking about PP men. You know, chomos."

"I, um, don't think you're allowed to say that."

"No! Not—"

Before Seeree could correct Baron, a filthy pink hand reached out from the bushes and grabbed Spot Velhalga.

"Clever ped," Seeree said under her breath.

The diminutive but adult-aged mushroom alien screamed for help as a second hand reached out from another bush. This hand initially looked darker than the first, but it was only because it was super hairy. Beneath the matted fur, the skin was even filthier/pinker. A third hand emerged from the bushes, followed by three more. Thirty-one fingers total (since one hand belonged to a polydactyl ped) tightened/glistened around Spot's no-no regions before pulling him, shrieking, into the dark foliage.

Jungle World (6-2)

"Just play along," Seeree muttered sternly. "We're too old to be on their radar. They probably thought Spot was a kid instead of a mushroom alien who's old enough to pay taxes. That obviously doesn't make what happened—what is likely still happening—to him okay, but it at least makes it a little less brutal. Oh yeah, plus I heard Spot say something racist earlier, so fuck him."

"Haha, I think we can call that box 'checked,'" Baron laughed.

"C'mon," Seeree snapped. "Be cool. We don't want to arouse any suspicion."

"Hey, I don't want to arouse frigg'n *anything* here."

"Exactly. We're totally outnumbered, and even my telekinetic powers won't be able to stop a panzer battalion of peds if they catch on that we're not one of them."

She grabbed Baron's hand and led him into the bushes, which were now covered in a viscous slime.

"Baller, it's that liquid lollipop stuff," Baron said. He released Seeree's hand and reached out at a strand. "I could use a quick sugar hit."

"No!" Seeree rasped. She re-grabbed Baron's hand. "That's not candy. Nothing in Jungle World is candy. They're legally not allowed to have it. Even on Halloween, they have to put signs on their doors that say, *No trick-or-treaters!*"

"Wow...they *are* monsters."

"Right. So, keep your head down and your mouth closed—for a couple of reasons."

She and Baron passed through to the other side of the bushes, where they saw a school bus, a smattering of cabins, and a lake that looked like it was composed of the same slime covering the leaves. A group of dumpy adults were skating across the lake's surface while humming the Charlie Brown theme.

"Eesh, what is this place?" Baron asked.

"This is Camp Chomowomo!" a voice replied. "Welcome!"

Baron and Seeree looked up and found themselves staring into the dewy, cargo-shorted crotch of an egg-shaped/middle-aged dude whose skin was the color of aged pink construction paper and the texture of a stretched-out balloon.

"Howdee dee, apple heads?!" he sang-said. "I'm Mr. Lester, the Head Counselor. That means I'm in charge of all the heads. First name, Childe."

"Childe Lester?!" Baron guffawed. "What's your middle name? Moe?!"

Seeree dug her fingernails into Baron's wrist.

"It's Pederast," Mr. Lester replied. "That was my mother's maiden name. Greek, or maybe Roman. We have family ties to both. But you two recruits can simply call me 'Counselor Lester.'"

"Recruits?" Baron asked warily.

"Yes, the new counselor recruits," Counselor Lester responded. He narrowed his piggish eyes. "You *are* the new recruits, aren't you?"

"Sure we are!" Seeree said while putting on her best ped affect. "This apple head just has a few soft spots. He's not the brightest cell in Protective Custody, you see."

"Well, that's fine," Counselor Lester said with a nod. "Doesn't take brains to be a counselor. Just takes a strong resolve, shockingly bare calves, and an ability to keep secrets. Damp hands don't hurt, either. Well, c'mon, let me give you a tour."

He helped Baron and Seeree up and led them across a field into a large mess hall.

"This here is our large mess hall," Counselor Lester explained as they entered. "This is where we make our *large* messes."

The smell was overpowering.

The lake/bush slime was everywhere.

"It's also where we host our Peenwood Derby Races," he continued.

"Don't you mean pinewood?" Seeree asked.

"No...I mean Peenwood. You know, you don't look much like a camp counselor, young recruit. You may share our supple, full cheeks, but your bosoms are all wrong. They're TOO big. And while our counselors are either extremely hairy or entirely hairless, with zero in-between, even the hairless ones have wispy mustaches. You don't. Yes, something about you is a bit...off."

"Oh, I'm definitely Chomowomo material," Seeree stammered. "I just, um, ate too much soy lecithin, so my bosoms became extra bosomy. Phytoestrogens, you know."

"I suppose that makes sense," Counselor Lester replied. "The bosoms being bosomy, I mean. I didn't understand that science stuff you said."

He turned to Baron, looked him up and down, and smiled. "Now, your fellow recruit, with that slightly asymmetrical face, tight potbelly, and those faded department store jeans—there's no question that HE is Camp Chomowomo material. A fine specimen, indeed! So, let's continue the tour. Like I said, this is where we make our *large* messes. For our *small-* and *medium*-sized messes, we tend to…"

"Seeree, what the shit?! I'm not a fucking ped!" Baron whispered as Counselor Lester led them past row after row of slime-encrusted cafeteria tables.

"I know that!" Seeree hissed. "But we need to play along until we find the boss. I can't waste my telekinetic powers beforehand, especially because you're useless without your guitar and with your tight pedbelly."

"Do you even know who the boss is?"

"And here," Counselor Lester continued while holding open a door at the end of the mess hall, "will be your sleeping…and *playing* quarters."

Baron and Seeree stepped back outside.

Even though it was daytime, the sunshine was sickly and dim, as if it were passing through a vaseline-covered film.

The perverted light shone upon hundreds of army-green tents packed tightly next to each other. They began to vibrate and ooze.

"We like to call this our *monster* mess hall," Counselor Lester said with a deranged smile. "AKA...The Tent City of Perverts."

"That's the boss," Seeree whispered fearfully.

"Yes, it is boss," Counselor Lester replied obliviously. "Boss and dandy."

Baron and Seeree followed the counselor into the tent city. Flaps parted, exposing unimaginable darkness within each interior.

"Don't look," Seeree warned as they passed a particularly slimy tent, but that only made Baron look faster.

In the tent, he saw the corpse of Spot Velhalga, encased in so much slime that it looked like he was in a cocoon. His face was plastered with a look of terror (and plastered with slime).

The counselor led Baron and Seeree into the heart of the Tent City of Perverts.

"Gentlepeds!" he said. "Come and welcome Camp Chomowomo's counselor recruits!"

"*Mmm,*" a thick wave of peds undulated hauntingly as they emerged from their tents.

"To celebrate," Counselor Lester said proudly, "please bring forth the sacrificial camper!"

From a nearby cabin, a figure was forcibly brought out by two refrigerator-sized peds wearing football helmets and too-tiny football jerseys. He was dressed in dinosaur pajamas and trembling like a can of paint (that's in a paint mixer, not just chilling on a shelf).

The pitiful figure was Garindax.

Jungle World
(6-💀)

Nevermind, it was just another mushroom alien.

Baron still didn't want to see it get touched, though, so he leaned over and whispered, "Seeree, use your frigg'n STEM powers already! We've found the boss, and even though I'm ripped, I can't take out a whole TCoP by myself!"

"No," Seeree hissed. "Not yet."

"Did this recruit just say '*No*'?" a frothing ped gasped.

"Yeah, and what's with that baby face?" another cried out. "Are you sure he's old enough to be a counselor? I think maybe he should be a *camper* instead!"

A muffled clicking reverberated through the trees as tips were pinched in unison/preparation.

"I...was just telling my fellow recruit here 'No, not yet,'" Seeree tried. "As in, 'It's not your turn to touch yet. I get to, um...touch first.'"

The peds sighed and nodded in relief, but the pinching continued.

"Very well," Counselor Lester said. "Please excuse our suspicion—and our razzing. And now, the time has come to strip down and don the ceremonial recruit uniforms."

He handed a black garbage bag to Baron, and another to Seeree.

"Strip?" Seeree asked hesitantly.

"Yes, you must forsake the clothing of the outside world and commit yourself to becoming one of us. Prove yourself like your fellow recruit!"

She turned to Baron, who was already naked and pushing his head/arms through the garbage bag because he just wanted to get Jungle World over with.

Seeree hesitantly removed her shirt and shorts.

A gasp echoed across the tents.

"The recruit's hairless body, fishnet stockings, and microscopic peen are par for the course," a brazen ped declared, "but his bosoms are all wrong! They're grotesquely large, inexplicably non-saggy, and where are the skin tags?!"

"Now, now, brothers," Counselor Lester answered, "I have spoken with the new recruit, and he assures me that his condition is simply a result of eating too much soy. Counselor Ceech, surely these bosoms are no greater than yours."

"Larger, perhaps, but surely no greater," a fat counselor with big boobs and hairy pepperoni nips exhaled.

"Despite your fellow recruit's commendable eagerness," Counselor Lester started. Seeree looked over at Baron, who was staring at her boobs and pitching his own garbage-bag tent. "I will grant your request and allow you the first touch." He waved a hand, and the football guards pushed the mushroom alien near her.

"Now, prove yourself," he continued. "Show us that you are more counselor than camper."

"Um, okay…" Seeree hesitated.

"Go on!" Counselor Lester said menacingly. "*Touch…or be touched.*"

"Hey, back off her!" Baron shouted. "She told you she's a ped, so she's definitely a ped, alright?!"

The counselors all leapt backwards and sneered, bearing their rotten fangs.

"SHE?!" they roared.

"Baron, dammit!" Seeree yelled.

"Seize them!" Counselor Lester yelled louder.

One of the football guards grabbed Baron, and the other grabbed Seeree.

"Close your eyes, and do your best with them, boys," Counselor Lester ordered the entire TCoP. "I want to see slime oozing from every orifice of their traitorous, disgusting bodies. Make new orifices if you have to."

"No fucking way!" Baron yelled.

He activated a jet boot and kicked backwards, nailing the football guard in his peen and melting it through his own butt.

He then slid over and rocket-kneed the other football guard so hard in the crotch that his balls launched into his helmet and made a little *ding!* sound like one of those carnival games.

Both guards collapsed to the ground and cried like little babies, which made the too-eager TCoP descend upon them and create new orifices until all that remained was slimy Swiss cheese.

Baron grabbed Seeree and the mushroom alien before blasting off into space with such fiery force that it torched every inch of Jungle World, killing all of the peds but also a shit-ton of wildlife.

Final World
(7-1)

"So, what was your top-secret STEM major plan back there?" Baron asked as Seeree walked into her living room to find him and the mushroom alien playing video games and eating chips.

"I...I didn't have enough power to take out the entire Tent City of Perverts," she said quietly while wrapping a towel around her hair. She had just taken a long/scalding shower and a long/cold look in the mirror. "So, I was going to telekinetically rip off the alien's clothes to send the peds into a frenzy."

"You what?!" the alien exclaimed.

"Then," she continued, "I was going to levitate him over a cliff so they'd chase after him and fall to their deaths."

"Dang!" Baron responded. "That would've ruled, minus the part about stripping my boy here. Why do you look like you feel so shit about it, though? Just because you choked and didn't do anything and almost got touched to death?"

"No. Because then I was going to drop the alien over the cliff, too."

"You what?!" the alien exclaimed again.

"We didn't need him," she explained. "We just needed the pin, and that would've been back in his hat. In his little clothes pile. From when I stripped him to use as ped bait before killing him. But none of that happened since you saved him. You saved both of us."

"Yeah, it was no big deal," Baron said nonchalantly. "I honestly wasn't even thinking about the pin. I just didn't want any of us to get put in a fucking slime cocoon like Spot Velhalga. Hey, guess what this guy's name is!"

"Spot Valhalga."

"Oh, bitch," Spot Valhalga snapped.

"It's not a hard pattern to figure out," Seeree said.

"Yeah, but we were still pumped to tell you," Baron said while crunching chips. "You don't always have to raid on everyone's parade."

"Rain."

"Right. Because that matters."

Baron unpaused and went back to his video game with Spot.

"Dude, this isn't the space chick you did a sex with, is it?" Spot whispered not-very quietly. "Please tell me it's not."

"Where's the pin?" Seeree demanded.

"Oh yeah, right here," Baron replied. He did a secret handshake with Spot Valhalga, who passed from the tip of his canoe/penis-shaped hat a glowing kidney stone shaped like a hilt with a hilt.

"Is that the last of them?" Baron continued. He tossed the pin to Seeree. "Because I'd really like to rescue Garindax now. Spot rules, but he's not that great at video games."

"There's one more," she said while sticking the pin onto her jacket. "In the final world. The only problem is, I'm not sure where that is."

"Oh, this is it," Spot said nonchalantly while playing video games. "This is where it all ends."

Final World (7-2)

"What do you mean, this is it?" Seeree gasped.

"Yeah, here in outer space," Spot replied while not looking up from the screen. "Space World *is* Final World."

"Space World? No, this is Planet Bookcase. This is normal. This is home. Everything *else* is outer space."

"Sure, to you," Spot continued. "To everyone else, *this* is outer space. Look at you. You're different than me. You're an alien. Baron, wouldn't you agree?"

"Oh, for sure," Baron replied. "Both of y'all are fucking weird."

"And so are you," Spot said. "Even though I love you like a brother. But if Seeree and I went to your planet, *it* would be 'fucking weird.' Your planet? Phew! Now that's outer space, man."

"No way," Baron said defensively. "Urth is super normal. It's boringly normal."

"Urth?" Spot exclaimed. "How do you even spell that? Right off the bat, that's crazy. It's alien. *You're* an alien."

"Nuh-uh."

"Tell me, then, how'd you get here?"

"In a rocket ship," Baron answered.

"Then how do you plan on getting back? Or better yet, how could I come visit you on Urth? What would I need?"

"A rocket shit. I mean, shit, a rocket ship."

"That's right. And wherever you fly a rocket ship *to* is outer-fucking-space. So, for me and everyone else, you're a Grade A alien, buddy."

"Wow…a alien," Baron whispered.

"*An* alien," Seeree corrected. "But that still doesn't explain who *you* are, Spot, or why you were in Jungle World, or why you're here eating my chips and probably farting into my couch."

"Doesn't it?" Spot said with a smile. He fired up a bowl and turned to Baron. "How long have you been into philosophy, man?"

"No," Seeree interjected pissedly. She walked over and turned off the TV. "It doesn't."

"Oh, bish, I hadn't saved," Spot whined.

"You're just a little stoner shithead," Seeree snapped. "So, get the fuck out of my apartment."

"Okay okay okay," Spot said as he was hurried out the door.

Final World
(7-💀)

"What the shit? You can just buy these pins online?" Seeree said while making a swiping motion on her phone.

"Whoa, that's crazy," Baron replied distantly even though he was chilling next to her on the couch and playing on Spot's save file.

"Yeah, look. All of these pins we collected are right here on this site. 'Pinhub.' Dumb name, but same-day shipping, and they're all super cheap."

"Oh damn, that's crazy," Baron replied. "You should definitely tell your boss that she said that about you."

"Look at this: World Seven pin. Five bucks. It'll be here in an hour, and sure enough, it's shaped like a mushroom alien who's smoking a blunt that also happens to be a hilt. Maybe Spot was onto something. Maybe this is the last world."

"Who?"

"Spot. Bohalfa? Valchamba? What was his name?"

"Spot, I think."

"Yeah. Heh heh. Hey, look at this video. It's a cat eating a cake, and then icing gets all over its whiskers."

"Whoa, damn," Baron said without looking up. "That's crazy."

"Now look at this one. After the ads. But this guy just bought his mom a brand-new hovercar. That's so cool. Seven million views, too, so he's definitely making a difference and helping a lot of people. It's pretty inspiring."

"Woof, damn, that's crazy."

Seeree continued swiping. "Um, did you add that mermaid bitch on Nerpbook?"

Baron's video game character tripped and fell into a pit of lava.

"Oh, um, yeah," he explained, "but only because we were working on a project together. It's a school thing."

"What 'school thing?' You're like a million years old and live on a different planet! Oh, and you added the genie bitches, too. Nice."

"Yeah, but, see, we were planning a surprise party for you, and—"

A knock at the door saved Baron's ass/balls.

Seeree opened it and found a package chilling on the ground.

A delivery hovercar with a license plate that read SPICYVEGINA was blazing away.

The mushroom alien driver didn't wave or tip his keyboard/wiener-shaped hat because he was too busy staring down at a screen to see where the next delivery was.

There was no epic boss battle, or interaction, or anything.

Seeree shrugged and opened the package.

The pin was much smaller than it looked online, there was a chip on the edge, it reeked of cigarettes, and there was a curly black hair in the bottom of the package.

Oh well, she thought. *At least it was cheap.*

"Okay. You want to go save Garindax and kill Dweem now?" she asked while plopping onto the couch and pinning the Seventh Pumpedly Pin to her jacket.

"In a minute," Baron replied. "First I gotta kill this alien. Sometimes he drops a better gun when you do, so then when you go to kill him again it's way easier."

"Why do you want to kill him again if you've already killed him?" Seeree asked.

"To get a better gun," Baron replied annoyedly. "I just said."

Seeree sighed and picked up Baron's phone by "mistake."

"What the fuck is a 'milking table,'" she demanded, "and why have you bookmarked, like, a million websites of it?"

Loading Screen
(. . . . .)

After Baron spent a couple hundred hours on his video game, and Seeree spent a couple hundred dollars on milking table streaming subscriptions, they began to experience boredom/carpal tunnel and decided to resume their adventure.

"Well, I guess we can both agree that this is outer space," Baron said as they blazed in Seeree's hovercar into black infinity.

"Yep, Dweem lives way the fuck out here in the spaceburbs," Seeree responded with one eye on the road and the other on her favorite streamer, i.e., her least favorite streamer whom she merely hate-watched. "He says it's because he needs quiet in order to concentrate on his creations, but between you and me he actually has so many restraining orders out against him that he can't live near, like, anyone."

"Stupid fucking Dweem," Baron growled. He had a flash of the spherical, innocent kid who burst into his life/kitchen covered in cookie crumbs and snowcone syrup.

Ultra Slaughterhouse. The precious cherub who used to love nothing more than watching cartoons, going on adventures, and making extra-heavy PBJs. The kid who would always try to give half of his PBJ to Baron and the other half to Garindax, in part because he sucked at math but also because he was as selfless as an orangutan.

Baron had felt so proud to have brought some pump into the world, and not just for himself.

Grandmas in every grocery store across Urth used to go nuts over Dweem, ruffling his hair and seeing how many knuckles they could fit into his cavernous bellybutton.

"How many knucks deep can I get in this young man?" they would ask while Baron bagged pears or something.

But now Dweem just hurt aliens like Seeree, took gross adult dumps, and created a bunch of stupid candy monsters that he almost definitely fucked physically, mentally, and/or emotionally before sending them out into the galaxy to hurt even more aliens.

Meanwhile, some other kid who was getting deep-knucked by grandmas and who would've grown up to be a cancer doctor got cancer instead fried eggs before he ever got the shot.

Baron stared into space, seeing all the darkness around the tiny, few stars.

"Oofa. Fucking cringe," Seeree laughed.

"What?" Baron asked defensively because he realized he probably looked pensive/baby.

"It's this milking table cringe comp," Seeree responded. "Some lady went to express this man's milk, but the table bent the wrong way, so the man started screaming. But then he farted, and then the director started screaming at everyone, but then he also farted. It's so bad, but so good."

Baron sighed and scanned the control panel in Seeree's hovercar for an ejection button. He found one and pressed it, but then he realized it was an LED screen displaying an ad for erection medicine. Now he was on their list.

Baron looked back into space and wondered how long it had been since he blinked.

I guess Dweem didn't ask to be born, he thought. *So, maybe it's not his fault. He was merely the product of fucking someone awful in a Party City dressing room on a monster planet.*

Baron remembered how excited he had been to take Leila to the Bone Zone in that dressing room. But then how as soon as he started thrusting for the two minutes it took to create life and simultaneously disappoint someone, he noticed "FUCK ALL MINGIES" carved in the bright blue paint of the dressing room wall. He fixated on it, wondering what "mingies" were, why someone hated them so much, and why they felt the need to share that hate. It was so angrily carved into the wall of an otherwise happy place that it almost caused him to lose his pump/bone. But Leila was new, and he was young, and it was all so easy to ignore back then.

Baron heard Seeree tell him to "check out this funny of another spooge and fart" as if he were a million miles underwater, where even those weird fish with translucent/sharp teeth and lightbulb dongs wouldn't dare approach because he looked like he had so little to lose, it would make them think about shit and go to church or something instead.

Baron counted five things he saw.

Four things he heard.

Three things he could feel.

Two things he could taste/smell.

One thing that was a fact at that moment.

Dweem's Keep (8-1)

"Wake up, little bish boy," a voice called.

"St. Wizzleteats?" Baron asked groggily. "Is it over? Is this Pumphalla?"

"No. It's the exact opposite: Dweem's Keep," Seeree replied.

Her eyes were bloodshot, and she was full of chai tea lattes and looking sweaty.

"Is that a fucking gun in your hand?" Baron as everything came back into troubling focus. "How many hours of milking table cringe comps did you watch?"

"It's not a gun. It's a red herring. And enough to get fired the fuck up." She pulled the hammer on a pistol. "C'mon, B, man, you ready? Let's go kill my brother."

"…My son."

"Haha yeah! That, too. Life is pretty weird, huh?"

"…But sometimes it's okay?" Baron tried.

"Jury's out on that one. But I can let you know when we're knucks deep in Dweem's writhing, steaming guts."

Dweem's Keep
(8-2)

Seeree killed the headlights as her hovercar busted up to a typical-looking suburban house floating in space.

"This is Dweem's Keep?" Baron asked. "It just looks like a normal house."

"That's a red herring, too. Look behind it."

Baron looked behind the house to find a two-car garage. Above it, a humongous gingerbread castle rose into infinity.

"*Fuuuuuuck*," Baron gasped. "Also, what's a red herring again?"

Seeree hovered the car up to the garage and killed the headlights.

She and Baron took deep breaths, held them so the space air wouldn't make them pop like skin/blood balloons, and then floated over to the top-secret side door that they learned about from *Space World Power* magazine.

"This still just seems like a normal garage," Baron said as he and Seeree found themselves in a narrow hallway lined with ladders, hammers, and gas canisters that smelled really fucking good.

"No shit, dummy," she replied. "Dweem doesn't live in the garage. He lives in the garage *apartment*."

She pointed to an ordinary looking wooden staircase that about halfway up turned into wrought-iron rotini. Machines, gears, and lava were everywhere, and the soundtrack changed from chill techno to intense industrial.

"See?" Seeree gloated. "I told you this was a final boss world."

She and Baron reached the top of the stairs and cautiously entered a white-walled, white-carpeted room. In the corner, a tiny CRT TV sat on the ground and glowed a sad blue.

On both sides of the TV rose pillars of lovingly stacked VHS cartoons and shitty 80s/90s PSAs. In front of them lay a solitary, squished pillow.

The airbrushed art on the pillowcase looked strangely familiar. Baron narrowed his eyes and made out a faded "Dweem Big—"

"Look, over there," Seeree exclaimed.

She pointed at another spiral staircase behind the TV.

But this one went down.

"What the shit?" Baron asked. "Why would Dweem make us go all the way to the top of his tower just to go back down another staircase? Won't this lead us back to the garage?"

"I don't think so," Seeree responded nervously. "If I know Dweem, these stairs must go *below* the garage. They most likely end in a basement…of some sort."

"Spooky," Baron whispered.

"Not really. It's just kind of dumb," Seeree replied. "I mean, who puts a basement access on the top floor? Dweem has always been weird like that. Mom used to think he had OCD or ADHD or something because he does weird shit like this and is really bad at eye contact and socializing and stuff. She tried removing gluten from his diet since she's a self-proclaimed mommy blogger and expert nutritionist, but it didn't do shit. But look who I'm telling. You're his frigg'n dad. Surely you noticed it when he lived with you?"

"I mean, I definitely noticed he was a little spaz baby. But me and Garindax would just yell at him, which seemed to work okay."

Baron and Seeree looked around the room at the crude crayon drawings on the walls. Most depicted broken guitars and bloodied but handsome metal musicians. Others portrayed boobs of various sizes/jigglinesses/species.

"Obviously," Seeree said. "C'mon. Let's go put this fuck out of his and our misery."

Dweem's Keep
(8-☠)

Baron and Seeree descended the second stairs and entered a cavernous, darkened chamber. In the center of the room loomed a solitary planet.

Above it, a large blue star glowed violently.

Below it, eight tiny purple stars glowed chilly.

The planet rotated on its axis: a shitty gaming chair purchased on Black Friday. The large star stopped streaming anime milking table videos.

A sun exploded above them.

Baron and Seeree's eyes focused on the sun, now merely a dangling lightbulb illuminating a hideous basement. The ceiling joists around the lightbulb were painted black, which they knew was a conscious color choice to hide mold before they could even smell it.

Then they fucking smelled it.

In the middle of the room, the planet rose from its still-very-overpriced throne.

"What took you so long?" the planet sighed.

"Ultra Slaughterhouse?!" Baron exclaimed, because now "Dweem" didn't fit this individual any better than 50-inch-waist slacks would have.

The planet-sized being wore a towering chef hat atop a greasy bowlcut, which remained free of gray hairs to show that not *too* much time had passed.

Beneath his bowlcut, a flaky brow furrowed, cold eyes narrowed, a glistening mustache curled, and yellow teeth clenched.

Beneath all that grossness, Dweem was in slightly better shape. He was still super fat, but he was also super ripped, with muscles and veins popping out all over his greasy chef apron and greasier chef arms. At the end of each arm was a hand capable of curling 75s with decent form and probably like 10 reps per set.

Neither hand was curling a dumbbell at that moment.

Instead, one hand gripped a meat cleaver.

The other gripped a guitar/spider monster.

"GARINDAX!" Baron shouted.

"BARON!" the eight blacklit stars shouted back.

Baron rushed toward his best friend in *EVERY* universe.

Mere inches from Garindax's glow-in-the-dark frets, however, he found himself restrained by a Swedish octopus.

"Ha!" Dweem chortled. "Forget it, Pops! You may have been able to push me around when I was just a kid, but now I'm in charge!"

"You're still just a kid to me" Baron replied. "The same little chub-chub who took a dump in the bathtub and then used it as shampoop. More importantly, though, you'll always be my son."

"Really?" Dweem asked dreamily. His eyes softened.

"Yep. And that means I can ground the fuck out of you anytime/anywhere."

"*Screeeee!*" Dweem shrieked as if someone had denied him Szechuan sauce. "Silence! I'm NOT your son anymore. I'm a frog now! I mean, a god! They call me the Candy Dandy! They call me Daddy Dulces! They call me Big Baby Sweets!"

"You're annoying as fuck, is what you are. How are you still alive, by the way? I'm pretty sure Garindax and I unexisted you with our wish to Santa back at Christmas Kingdom, right before he started stacking it and jacking it."

"Technically, it was just Baron who wished it," Garindax clarified.

"True," Baron nodded. "But, yeah, how are you still alive? And how many reps do you do for curls? Do you partials? Do you do like a rotating thing where some days you max out with low weight at like 35 reps, and then other days you max out with high weight at like three reps? Do you do partials? I think I already asked you that. But if not, do you do partials?"

"There are more things in outer space and Urth, Father, than are dreamt of in your philosophy," Dweem replied with an arrogant smirk. "That's from ICP, by the way. But why are you asking *me* for workout advice? I'm just a 'nudnik.' Isn't that what you used to called me? Or was it a 'Budnick from Salute Your Shorts'?"

"Haha, man we rule," Baron cracked up.

"No joke," Garindax laughed back.

"A failure. A disappointment. A mistake," Dweem trailed off.

"Dude, we were just goofing," Baron said.

"Well, now the goof is on you, you literal motherfucker. Of my mom, not yours. I love grandma. But you did fuck my mother."

"Ah, shit," Baron sighed. "Don't tell me you have mom issues, too."

Dweem lifted Garindax by the guitar neck and raised the meat cleaver, which under the dim light Baron could tell was actually a cleaver-shaped guitar pick.

"When you get to Pumphalla," Dweem said menacingly, "you can ask Saint Wizzleteats at the Pumpedly Gates about my issues. And about who caused them. And about the benefits of doing partials."

"Baron, look out!" Garindax warned. "He's been watching F-You-Tube guitar tutorials!"

"I learned how to create life," Dweem said quietly, "and then I learned how to take it away. And now I've learned…to take it away. That's slightly different, by the way. First I said, 'I learned *how* to take it away,' but then just straight 'I've learned to take it away.' That means the world made me this way. I'm like the Joker."

"Yeah, the 2019 version. Contrived/cringey," Baron replied.

"Haha oh my fuck!" Garindax laughed.

Dweem palm-muted him, and then he fretted a greasy power chord.

"Badbye, Pops," he said with a smile.

Dweem's Keep
(8-💀-💀)

Baron closed his eyes, bummed that he was about to fry eggs, but relieved that it would technically be by Garindax's fangs.

"Drop it, Fuckface Jr.," Seeree shouted, busting out from the shadows behind Baron and cocking her gun.

"Seeree!" Dweem and Garindax shouted at the same time.

"That's right, I—wait, how does the guitar know who I am?"

"Dweem talks about you *a lot*," Garindax replied. "Plus, he has two massive folders on his desktop: one is called *Seeree Fakes*, which is like 10 gigabytes, and the other one is called *Seeree Deepfakes*, which is like 31 terabytes. You, um, definitely don't want to see what's in either of those. Do you know what a 'milking table' is?"

"Shhshhshh," Dweem hissed.

"Fucking gross," Seeree shuddered. "Anyway, drop it, Fuckface Jr."

"Drop what?" Dweem asked. "Garindax, or my cleaver pick?"

"Dude, it doesn't matter. Just drop one of them or I'll shoot."

"The pick!" Baron suggested.

"You don't have the guts," Dweem said with a confident smile.

"No," Seeree said coolly while the camera zoomed in and the music cut out. "But you do."

She fired the gun at Dweem's colossal stomach.

Before the bullet even left the chamber, Dweem strummed the power chord to fire an electric spiderweb from Garindax's fangs.

The web wrapped around the gun, causing the bullet to backfire.

"Fuck!" Seeree yelled as the barrel exploded in her hand.

"Hey…now there's an idea," Dweem said.

He summoned another Swedish octopus, but this one had more drool and phallic tentacles. It wriggled around Seeree, trapping her while also acting like a corset.

"Now, what'd you say?" he rasped. "Drop it? Sure thing. I need a free hand to *pinch tips/nips*."

"Oof," Baron grunted. "I really, really wish I had pulled out in that Party City dressing room."

Dweem ignored him and dropped the cleaver pick, while maintaining a tight grip on Garindax with his other hand.

The planet-sized creep loomed over Seeree, who struggled against the Swedish octopus while making little anime yelping sounds and squishing her boobs together.

"Don't feel bad," Dweem whispered with hot breath that smelled like a cocktail of coconut milk and sardines.

"You gave it your best shot, but I'm a superior being with a superior intellect: A gentle sir who schooled himself in the dark arts while you were figuring out how to do that cat-eye makeup thing. Why don't you do that anymore, by the way? I liked that. Anyway, after ages of mastering bating and candymancy, it's finally time to get me some *sweet*."

Dweem's Keep
(8-💀-💀-💀)

Dweem licked his lips and leaned in for the kiss/kill. But then, he stopped.

"What…what are those?" he gasped while staring directly at her chest.

"Take a closer look," Seeree said slyly. She did some more anime noises and ahegao faces, but this time it was obviously a put-on.

"Is that a frigg'n…a *fucking* World 1 pin?" Dweem stammered. "And a World 2 pin?!"

"Keep going."

Dweem released his tip, as there was nothing left to pinch. He had gone entirely concave.

"*3, 4, 5, 6, ohyoubitch, SEVEN PINS?!*"

"That's right," Seeree replied. "I'm glad they at least taught you counting in culinary school."

"How long did it take you?"

"How long did it take to do *what?*" she replied knowingly.

"HOW FUCKING LONG DID IT TAKE YOU TO GET THE PINS?!" Dweem demanded.

"Oh, that? I really don't know," Seeree sighed while shooting a glance at her smartwatch.

Dweem grabbed her wrist and pulled the watch to his bulging eyebrains.

"Three days!?" he shouted. "Chocolate World ALONE takes that long! You got all of the pins in three days?! One weekend?!"

"If that's what it says," Seeree replied with a hair flip. "To be honest, I don't worry about stuff like that. I'm more into collecting pins for *fun*."

"Bitchwhoreliar," Dweem snapped, throwing her wrist down.

"Okay, okay, okay," he repeated while rubbing his temples and waddling back over to the large star, i.e., his computer screen. He crashed into his chair and began frantically scrolling on a website called *Space Worlds Done Quick*.

"And this was glitchless, no warp?" he asked in a total panic.

"Yep," Seeree said.

He scrolled. His eyelid started to twitch.

"And, obviously, you didn't use Game Genie, or Game Shark, or *buy* any of the pins?" he asked with a glimmer of hope.

"Nope," Seeree lied. "It was a 100% legit run. I guess I could submit it to SWDQ if I wanted to. Who has the best speedrun time right now? Some tubby/virginal mama's boy?"

"Shut up, shut up, shut up! I need to think."

Seeree narrowed her eyes. Her nose started to bleed.

"Almost…" she whispered.

Dweem started rocking back and forth in his computer chair, like, *big time.*

He grabbed one of his thighs with his free hand and began clawing into it with his fingernails. He reached for his other thigh but realized he was still holding Garindax.

He hesitated for a moment, and his jaw did a little spasm thing, but then he released his grip.

Garindax clattered to the sticky ground as Dweem immediately went to town on his thighs and chair rocking.

"Now!" Seeree yelled.

"I still can't do anything," Baron said because he was ensnared by a Swedish octopus.

"I know," Seeree replied. "I was just yelling to get myself pumped."

"Fart yeah," Baron and Garindax said at the same time.

"Man, I missed you," they said to each other again at the same time.

Seeree telekinetically unraveled the phallic Swedish octopus tentacles wrapped around her, turned them backward, and made the candy cephalopod 8P itself with no slime lube right in the mouth/butt/lady parts (because it was actually a lady Swedish octopus, so maybe don't assume stuff).

She then telekinetically lifted Garindax off the ground and flew him over to Baron in slow motion.

Baron and Garindax's ten eyes widened, and their bodies became respectively covered in more goosebumps/guitarbumps with every second that they grew nearer.

As they finally reconnected, every single note hammered-on and then pulled-off, causing a pumpsplosion of maximum intensity.

The gummy octopus holding Baron immediately melted into infinity tentacles that turned and ∞P'd themselves with no slime lube right in the mouth/butt (because it was a dude).

Baron picked up Garindax, who immediately rubbed his headstock all over his buddy's chest in order to mark him with his scent.

"Haha! Take it easy, buddy!" Baron laughed. "Don't worry, we're best friends forever again! And double don't worry, because I never played video games with alien mushroom monsters or told them they were my best friends forever!"

Garindax stopped marking Baron. "Uh, that was oddly specific. Seems like something that we should maybe have a conversation about?"

"Not now, ladies!" Seeree shouted.

"Wow, okay, *rudeness*. Who's this bish again?" Garindax asked.

"Dweem's sister," Baron responded.

"You're shitting me! She's not your daughter, is she?"

"Nah. We thought she was for like an hour or two before realizing she wasn't. She's Leila's kid, so I guess she's technically Dweem's half-sister, but my nada. As soon as we—mostly—figured that out, we did a sex, boobs and everything. It was dope."

"Damn, that is dope. But it's still fucked up that she's Dweem's half-sister. You should hear the shit he said about her…the erotic fanfics he wrote. It's more than just half-creepy."

"Yeah, what's this dude's deal? And what did y'all do all weekend?"

"Pretty much this."

"Yeesh."

"You're telling me. I kept thinking about how you probably should've just pulled out in that Monsteropolis Party City dressing room."

"Dude, same!"

"Haha, crew. Man, I'm so glad we're chilling again."

"Me too, homie. Oh, yeah, did you at least see his workout routine? Did he do partials?"

"LADIES?!" Seeree yelled.

Dweem's rocking was beginning to chill.

"Okay," he mumbled, "maybe I can save a few frames if I equip the garbage bag counselor armor *before* spawning in Jungle World, like at the end of Ice World. But then I'd have lower couth stats, so Queen Areola wouldn't even address me. Fuck. So, that's out. Maybe I can figure out a way to clip directly into the Tent City of Perverts, skipping the large mess hall cutscene and small mess hall quick time events. Skipping the...LMH CS and the SMH QTEs. Would that count as a glitchless run, though? Fuck!"

"Play a chord or a scale or something, Baron!" Seeree shouted. "Finish him! Quickly!"

"Uh..." Baron hesitated.

He fingered a barre chord and aimed it at Dweem, whose rocking/clawing had painfully picked back up.

Tiny gumdrop monsters spawned across his computer desk and spun around aimlessly. A taffy professor grew from behind the monitor and counted frames before another spawned next to him and counted a different number of frames. They began fighting. A honey bun alien spawned on top of the keyboard and tried to say something inspirational to everyone, but when it realized no one was listening started to cry and eat itself. Dweem conjured a brownie cover for his gaming chair followed by a weighted blanket of icing that gently spread itself across his chef apron.

His costume.

"I...don't think he's really that big of a threat," Baron said, unfretting the chord.

"Yes, he is!" Seeree shouted. "He makes these stupid monster candy things! I don't like them! No one likes them! I don't like *him*! Just kill him!"

"Nah, now that I got Garindax back, we'll probably just bail. Chungin' the deuce!" Baron said as he turned to the door.

"Chocolate deuce!" Garindax called from Baron's back.

"Haha, so good because it's a big candy adventure, but also because it could be a poop reference."

As Baron stepped on the first stair of the stairs leading upstairs, the stairs crumbled into a pile of stairs.

He and Garindax spun around slowly, but with panache.

"You're not going anywhere," Seeree said menacingly as a drop of blood fell from her nose.

Dweem's Keep
(8-💀-💀-💀-💀)

"What's your deal?" Baron demanded.

"I can't let you leave until you've killed your son," Seeree replied.

"Why do you *really* want Dweem killed?" Baron doubly-demanded. "You can't hate his candy creations that much. Look, you're eating a divinity flying eyeball monster right now, and you and I both know those are good as fuck. Is it because of all the fakes, deepfakes, fanfics, and probably the custom RealDoll he made of you? That's no big deal! If ladies and dudes had *any* idea how many people took care of business thinking about them, everyone would be walking around in hazmat suits or with fully erect wieners/nips. So, out with it. What's the cool twist?"

"Okay, fine," Seeree sighed. "I'll level with you."

"You better *final level* with me," Baron said while looking back to Garindax for approval.

"Haha, sheer brilliance," Garindax laughed.

"Shut up!" Seeree snapped. "I'm glad the guitar wasn't on our adventure. But, like I was saying, I'll level with you. Better yet, I'll split it with you. You know how Dweem used to let grandmas go knucks deep on him in grocery stores?"

"Yeah, I was thinking about that during the drive over here," Baron replied. "But that was when he was a little kid. Well, he was never little, but he was a kid. You probably weren't even born yet. So, how do you know about it? And how old are you, exactly?"

"It doesn't matter. What does matter is that Dweem wasn't doing it to be a cute, innocent fat. He was ingratiating his way into all of their wills."

"Whoa, crazy. Hey, guess what else is crazy? Garindax said he saw a deepfake video of you doing milking table to *yourself.*"

"Gross. But that means Dweem was only being nice to the grandmas so they would give him their money when they die. He's fucking loaded. How do you think he has time to just sit on ass, playing video games and making candy creations?"

"Oh, motherfucker…"

"And because he's so obsessed with me and he doesn't have any friends," Seeree continued, "I'm listed as the primary beneficiary for when he dies. Obviously, though, there's a clause stating that if I kill him, I don't get shit. So, I need you to kill him. We'll split the money 50-50. And I'll do hand stuff on you as a reward/treat."

"Okay," Baron said. "But we split it 64-31. And you have to do hand stuff on Garindax."

"But he's a guitar. And what the fuck is that math?"

"Slash spider monster, so he has pink thing. And those numbers rule more than 50."

"Fine, but I get the 64. And can I do telekinetic stuff on him instead of hand stuff?"

"Fine, I actually wanted 31. That's Halloween. And only if I can telekinetically kill Dweem, which you know I can't acause there's no ADHD in STEM. So, it's all hands on deck/pink thing."

"Alright, fuck it. Deal. But you also have to stop saying 'acause.'"

"Applesauce. That means 'deal.'"

"Are you killing him or not?" Seeree sighed.

"Yo, we can't do telekinetic *or* hand stuff with her," Garindax whispered. "We're both married."

"Shhshhshh," Baron hissed.

"What was that?!" Seeree exclaimed.

"Oh, he was just wondering if a mushroom alien is going to bust in after we kill Dweem," Baron lied. "Like, will there be another pin for this world, or just the credits with smooth jazz playing while we stack it and jack it?"

"I hope there isn't another one," Seeree said. "The mushroom alien who gave us the World Seven pin was named Spicy Vegina, or at least that was the license plate on his delivery truck. So, following the pattern, the next one would be—."

"*DELIVERY TRUCK?!*" Dweem exploded.

He spun around so quickly/pissedly that his icing blanket melted and the brownie chair cover turned into chocolate charcoal.

"That's cheating!" he shrieked. "Not glitchless! Not a record!"

"Oh fartknockers..." Baron, Garindax, and Seeree muttered together.

Dweem loomed over them.

He spawned two humongous peanut brittle meat cleavers that were *actual* meat cleavers, not guitar picks. The handles alone were easily 25 pounds, and the blades were 50.

He began curling them with minimal effort.

Seeree tried to telekinetically rip them from his hands, but that only caused Dweem to grip them harder. His form improved.

"Thanks for the spot, babe," he laughed.

With each rep, the blades grew closer.

Baron slung Garindax over his shoulder and wailed a quick thrash melody, which shot neon icicles into the handles and added at least another ten pounds each.

Dweem struggled to continue his set. His arms froze.

Baron, Seeree, and Garindax sighed in relief—but then gasped in horror.

Dweem was doing partials.

"Oh my fuck," the trio gasped.

There was nothing they could do.

As the cleavers hung inches from their heads, then centimeters, then micrometers or whatever, a mechanical explosion shook the basement. The walls began to implode, letting in the cold black inkiness of space.

Dweem's Keep
(8- 💀 - 💀 - 💀 - 💀 - 💀)

Everyone held their breath and focused on the expanding void.

Suddenly, a shadowy figure appeared on the other side. Mysterious fog enveloped the creature. On top of its head, a tentacle or possibly a wiener wobbled in the dark.

"Oh, fart! Is that my best friendo in the universe, Sam Vahelta?!" Baron yelled. "Come to rescue us/chill?"

"What the fuck? Best friendo in the universe?" Garindax asked dejectedly.

"It can't be Sam Vahelta," Seeree explained, "because I killed his dumbass."

"Hi, I'm about to kill all your dumbasses," Dweem said while machine-gun-repping partials.

"Oh, yeah, you did kill Sam," Baron said, ignoring Dweem. "Both of them. They frigg'n ruled, too."

"Just how many new best friends did you make while Dweem was struggling to learn how to play Star Light Zone on me?" Garindax demanded.

"Well, maybe it's a new mushroom alien monster," Baron continued to Seeree. "Maybe it's Snot Vahalfa."

"Can't be," she said. "The last one was named 'Spicy Vegina.' It's X Y, where X is the first name and Y is the last name, and for each pair, only the second letter of Y changes from 'e' to 'a.' So, it goes First *Lest*, First *Last*. Which means this is—"

"SPICY VAGINA!" Baron, Garindax, and Dweem shouted together excitedly.

"What the FUCK did you call me?" a pissed mom voice cut through the basement.

Recessed lights blasted on throughout the room, illuminating far more than the one dumb, dangling lightbulb that Dweem chilled beneath because he was too lazy to flip a switch.

Outside of the disgusting computer station, the rest of the basement (i.e., the converted garage), was super nice. There was plush carpet, a pair of couches set up theater style so one was higher than the other, and a projector mounted to the ceiling. A nice projector, not some $69 "HAYKO HD 2160P 8D OKAY USA" online bullshit.

Against the back wall was a minifridge of soda/beer/energy drinks/ice pops. On top of the fridge sat a hopper filled with Goldfish, with divided compartments so you could choose from pizza, cheese, or a "swirl."

A slightly older, more professional and still remarkably babe version of Seeree walked in through an open garage door. A ponytail bobbed on top of her head, and in her arms she held a tray of Hot Pockets that were steaming like crazy.

"Leila!" Baron and Garindax yelled.

"Mom!" Dweem and Seeree yelled.

"Oh my frog, how the fuck did you find out where I live?" Leila asked exhaustedly.

"Seeree invited me," Baron replied.

"Of course. I should've known. She's going through this whole rebellious tween phase."

"Yoooooo what the shit?!"

"I'm not a tween, Mom!" Seeree interjected. "I'm not even a teenager anymore. You might've known that if you weren't always on your stupid book tours. *Eating Twisty* and *Eating Twisty 2: Eating Twistier!* More than a bojojillion copies sold, rivaling only Quilted Hyper Plush as the most widely distributed toilet paper this side of the Box-of-Tissues-for-Masturbation Nebula."

"Watch it, Miss Bish," Leila snapped. "Those 'stupid book tours' paid for your STEM classes. Honestly, I don't know why you insisted on studying that nonsense instead of following in my and your brother's culinary footsteps."

"You copy/paste recipes from the internet, and Dweem makes monsters! Plus, you're a self-proclaimed expert nutritionist, but here you are with a platter of Hot Pockets. In case you haven't noticed, your son is fat as fuck!"

"Um, excuse you," Dweem said in a much babier voice. "But I'm actually in a bulking phase right now. That said, mother, I shall gladly accept those piping-hot bad boys." He dropped the weights and sauntered over to Leila.

"You're just in time, by the way," he said with a mouthful of pepperoni and a handful of mom dress. "Seeree and Da—er—*Baron* were about to ravage me. They even said something about having Garindax do 'pink thing' stuff to my body. That's the only reason anime milking table videos are on the computer screen. They forced me to watch them. It was part of their plan to groom me and then hook me on drugs. They wanted your precious son to be subject to, and reliant upon, their and anyone else's salacious desires."

"You fucking liar!" Seeree yelled while Baron and Garindax wondered what 'salacious' meant. "He was about to kill us!"

"You were about to kill me!" Dweem sobbed. "But first you said you were going to glue your hand to my butt—to my bare bottom and for an indeterminate time or purpose. Mother, it was absolutely harrowing!"

"I'm here now, baby," Leila said while stroking Dweem's greasy locks. "I'm here."

She turned to Baron and Garindax. "But I'm not sure why you still are."

Baron shrugged, slung Garindax over his back, and bailed out into the driveway. Through a window of the red-brick/red-herring house, a vampire dad in a business suit stood in the middle of a fancy kitchen. He shook his head and closed the fancy wooden slat blinds.

Baron turned back around, but the garage door was already closing. What moments before had been a spooky basement now cast the only visible light from the few inches that remained open.

The light disappeared and Leila, Dweem, and Seeree went silent as the door shut with a loud *clank*.

He turned into the dark and walked down a hard cement driveway.

At the end of it stood a streetlight, glowing yellow and re-illuminating the night. Its spotlight fell upon a neatly edged lawn. An anthill rose from a crack in the sidewalk. A car drove past. Drove into the neon green sky.

As the sound of the car faded into the distance, he heard crickets chirping. A train whistled in the distance. A mosquito buzzed by his ear and landed on his neck.

It bit him, but it didn't hurt. It felt familiar. The summer air was humid. It felt familiar, too. In spite of the heat, he zipped up his hoodie and stuck his hands into the front pockets.

He stepped off the curb and onto the street. His sneakers plodded against the asphalt as he walked in the opposite direction of the car. It had seemed like the car was heading home, and he wasn't ready yet. He hoped to find out where it had come from. Maybe a grocery store. He could go for a cold soda—something red—and a cheap, ovenwaveable pizza. He could almost taste them.

He didn't know for sure if there would be a store on the way, but that was okay.

It was fun to walk at night.

The moon was high, so it must've been late.

There wouldn't be any more cars on the street. Certainly not any more people. But the houses lining both sides remained filled with life. Through glowing windows, families watched TV, ate dinner, and read books.

He liked to imagine what they were watching, eating, and reading. Maybe it was something he would enjoy. Maybe they weren't so different. Maybe he wasn't.

Through a window, a cat looked at him and blinked slowly. Through another, a dog wagged its tail excitedly.

There was one night a year where he would've stopped and gone up to the houses.

Talked to the families.

Pet the cats and dogs.

Not worried about having to make eye contact or shake anyone's hand because his eyes were hidden, and his hands were covered.

Been rewarded for the successful interaction before doing it over and over again until his legs or the clock gave out.

He smiled and continued walking.

Tonight wasn't that night.

But it would be back.

Some Monkid's Bedroom

"Wait, so that's it?"

"Yep."

"Baron was a kid the whole time?"

"I, um, I don't know. I *hope* he wasn't an adult who trick-or-treats while hiding his age behind a mask and gloves. That'd be weird."

"Super weird, and gross. But what happened to Garindax? And Dweem and Seeree?"

"He didn't say. Maybe he never existed. Maybe none of them did. What was that about a hoodie? Could you zip up a hoodie with a guitar on your back? That seemed intentional. Honestly, though, I just don't think he knew how to end it."

"Oh, well. At least we got the video game."

"Yep. And at least I got the high score."

"Mondad?"

"Yes, monson?"

"You never said, 'The End.'"

"The End."

Made in the USA
Middletown, DE
31 July 2021